LOVE AND BULLETS

Fargo and Roxanne were breathless in bed, covered with a fine sheen of sweat. The breeze that fluttered the curtains felt mighty good, Fargo thought. His eyes strayed in that direction. . . .

The curtains fluttered again, a little too much this time. Fargo clamped an arm tightly around Roxanne as instinct galvanized his muscles. He rolled swiftly toward the edge of the bed, taking her with him. His other hand shot out and closed around the butt of the Colt where it protruded from the holster on the bedside table.

As Roxanne yelped in alarm and they tumbled off the bed with their arms still around each other, shots blasted from the window and heavy slugs tore through the mattress where they were an instant before. . . .

THE
TRAILSMAN
#286

TEXAS
TERROR TRAIL

by

Jon Sharpe

Ⓞ
A SIGNET BOOK

SIGNET
Published by New American Library, a division of
Penguin Group (USA) Inc., 375 Hudson Street,
New York, New York 10014, USA
Penguin Group (Canada), 90 Eglinton Avenue East, Suite 700, Toronto,
Ontario M4P 2Y3, Canada (a division of Pearson Penguin Canada Inc.)
Penguin Books Ltd., 80 Strand, London WC2R 0RL, England
Penguin Ireland, 25 St. Stephen's Green, Dublin 2,
Ireland (a division of Penguin Books Ltd.)
Penguin Group (Australia), 250 Camberwell Road, Camberwell, Victoria 3124,
Australia (a division of Pearson Australia Group Pty. Ltd.)
Penguin Books India Pvt. Ltd., 11 Community Centre, Panchsheel Park,
New Delhi - 110 017, India
Penguin Group (NZ), cnr Airborne and Rosedale Roads, Albany,
Auckland 1310, New Zealand (a division of Pearson New Zealand Ltd.)
Penguin Books (South Africa) (Pty.) Ltd., 24 Sturdee Avenue,
Rosebank, Johannesburg 2196, South Africa

Penguin Books Ltd., Registered Offices:
80 Strand, London WC2R 0RL, England

First published by Signet, an imprint of New American Library,
a division of Penguin Group (USA) Inc.

First Printing, August 2005
10 9 8 7 6 5 4 3 2 1

The first chapter of this book previously appeared in *Salt Lake Slaughter,* the
two hundred eighty-fifth volume in this series.

PUBLISHER'S NOTE
This is a work of fiction. Names, characters, places, and incidents either are
the product of the author's imagination or are used fictitiously, and any resem-
blance to actual persons, living or dead, business establishments, events, or
locales is entirely coincidental.
    The publisher does not have any control over and does not assume any
responsibility for author or third-party Web sites or their content.

The Trailsman

Beginnings . . . they bend the tree and they mark the man. Skye Fargo was born when he was eighteen. Terror was his midwife, vengeance his first cry. Killing spawned Skye Fargo, ruthless, cold-blooded murder. Out of the acrid smoke of gunpowder still hanging in the air, he rose, cried out a promise never forgotten.

The Trailsman they began to call him all across the West: searcher, scout, hunter, the man who could see where others only looked, his skills for hire but not his soul, the man who lived each day to the fullest, yet trailed each tomorrow. Skye Fargo, the Trailsman, the seeker who could take the wildness of a land and the wanting of a woman and make them his own.

Texas, 1860—
Where twisting trails are filled
with deception and danger.

1

The woman—or trouble?

That was the question Skye Fargo had to ask himself as he stood at the bar of the Fort Worth saloon and sipped from a mug of beer.

Of course, philosophically speaking, women often *were* trouble, Fargo thought, but at the moment he wasn't interested in philosophy. His attention was directed more toward the long, midnight-black hair and graceful yet sensuous curves of the young woman who stood next to him.

He had ridden into Fort Worth about half an hour earlier, a big man in buckskins on a magnificent black-and-white Ovaro stallion. He had ridden in from the piney woods of East Texas and was glad to get out of that humid, mosquito-infested country.

In the cross timbers region of north central Texas, Fort Worth had grown up around the army post of the same name that had been founded about a dozen years earlier. Now it was a good-sized crossroads town. Fargo had passed through it several times in the past and knew the best places to cut the trail dust from his throat.

As dusk settled, he left the Ovaro tied at the hitch rail outside and entered the Top Notch Saloon on Commerce Street intent only on getting a drink, and maybe later a meal. If there was a good poker game going on, he might sit in on that, too.

But he had been in the saloon only a short time when he noticed a young man standing several feet away along the bar, tossing back shots of whiskey. He was old enough to drink, but he couldn't have had much experience at it.

He seemed bound and determined to make up for that, however. He was bleary-eyed and none too steady on his feet, and his voice was more blurred every time he ordered another round. He wore town clothes, and his collar seemed to be too tight. He kept tugging at it.

Fargo made it a rule not to stick his nose into other people's business unless he was invited, and even then he was wary about it. If that young fella wanted to drink himself into a sodden state, that was his affair.

But then Fargo's lake-blue eyes, which were noted for their keenness all across the West, saw how three roughly dressed men at a corner table were watching the youngster. Their expressions were of cruel anticipation and avarice.

When the boy left the saloon, the trio of hard-cases intended to follow him, jump him, and rob him. Fargo was as sure of that as if he had overheard them talking about it.

Again, it was none of his business, but there was a chance they might really hurt the youngster, even kill him. Fargo was going to have a hard time doing nothing when he knew that possibility existed.

Then the girl had come along to complicate things.

Her name was Roxanne, she told him. She had a place upstairs where she would surely admire to take him and show him a good time.

Fargo had been a while without a woman, and he was a man of vast appetites for many things, including female companionship. So he was sorely tempted.

"What do you say, honey?" she cajoled as she looked up at him with appealing green eyes. She rested a hand on his arm and rubbed it in little circles.

From this angle, Fargo had a good view down the low-cut neckline of her spangled dress. He could see most of the firm globes of lightly freckled flesh, down to the brown upper edges of her nipples.

Movement that he caught from the corner of his eye made him look around. He saw the young boozer stumbling toward an empty table, glass in hand. The fella sat down, drained the drink, and then slowly slumped forward until his head was resting on the table. A snore came from his mouth.

Fargo smiled faintly. The boy had finally shown a little sense. He wouldn't be going anywhere for a while.

"Well, what about it?" Roxanne prodded.

"Lead the way," Fargo told her.

Roxanne laughed and took hold of his hand. "I thought you were gonna make me wait all night, darlin'."

"Plenty of other men in here," Fargo commented.

She laughed again. "None of 'em that look like you, though."

Fargo wasn't vain, but he was realistic. He knew that women found his rugged good looks attractive. He didn't try to take advantage of that, but he didn't ignore it, either. With Roxanne's hand in his, he climbed a narrow set of stairs to the second floor.

A balcony overlooked the main room of the saloon, and off that balcony were small bedchambers where Roxanne and the other girls plied their

3

trade. She opened the door to one and led Fargo inside.

The furnishings consisted of a bed—the sheets looked relatively clean, Fargo noted with approval—a chair, and a small table with a lamp and a basin on it. The lamp was already lit, the flame turned low.

After closing the door, Roxanne turned the lamp up, and its yellow glow filled the room. She turned her back to Fargo, lifted her long black hair, and said rather coyly, "Would you unbutton my dress?"

Fargo was glad to oblige. As the back of the dress came open, he slid it down over her shoulders. Roxanne pulled her arms out of the sleeves, wiggled her hips, and pushed the dress down over her thighs. It fell to the floor around her feet.

That left her wearing only stockings and slippers. She turned to face Fargo. She hadn't been in this game long enough for it to wear on her. She was still young, fresh, and beautiful. Her breasts were high and full and firm, crowned by dark brown nipples. The thatch of hair between her legs was as dark as that on her head.

She came into Fargo's arms and tilted her head up for his kiss. Her lips parted eagerly under the probing caress of his tongue. He rested one hand on the smooth skin between her shoulder blades while the other slid down her back to the curve of her hips.

She surged against him, molding her body to his through the buckskins he wore. His shaft quickly grew hard, and she slipped a hand between them to caress it. A low moan came from deep in her throat as she explored him and realized how much of him was waiting for her.

She drew her head back and gasped, "Oh, my God, Skye! I can't wait!"

4

He bent slightly, slipped an arm around the backs of her thighs, and straightened, picking her up and slinging her face down over his shoulder. That put her lovely rump right next to his ear. He gave it a little slap as he turned around and walked over to the bed.

Then, with one swift, unexpected movement, he dumped her on the mattress and said, "I'm afraid you're going to have to wait a while, Roxanne."

Then he turned to the door.

"What . . . what are you doing?" she exclaimed as she sprawled nude, lovely, and confused on the bed. "Where are you going?"

"There's something I have to do," Fargo told her over his shoulder. "Stay right there."

He didn't know if she would do as he told her or not, but right now, he didn't care. He stepped out onto the balcony and his eyes swept the crowded room below him.

Just as he expected, the young man who had been drinking so heavily was no longer dozing at the table. Nor was he to be seen anywhere else in the saloon.

As Fargo stood there, his hands clenched on the balcony railing, a shot blasted somewhere in the night outside the saloon. The hubbub inside the Top Notch muffled the sound, but Fargo heard and recognized it.

His long legs took him to the stairs and then down, two at a time. When he reached the bottom he started across the room, shouldering men out of the way, ignoring their angry, startled reactions. He made it to the door and slapped the batwings aside. Pausing as he stepped onto the boardwalk, he listened intently.

The sounds of a struggle, accompanied by harsh voices raised in anger, came from a dark patch of shadows to his right. As he came to the black mouth of an alley, he heard a man bark, "Watch it! Grab him, damn it! He's getting away!"

Running footsteps pounded toward Fargo. As his eyes adjusted to the darkness, he saw a figure loom up from the shadows and stagger toward him. But then the man's feet got tangled up with each other and he pitched forward, slamming hard to the ground.

The impact must have stunned the fleeing man, because he didn't move. Three more shapes appeared behind him, closing in.

"Now we've got him," one of the men growled.

Fargo took a step toward them and said, "No, what you've got is trouble."

The three men stiffened. Fargo had no doubt that they were the hardcases he had seen in the saloon, just as he was certain the man lying senseless on the ground was the youngster who had been pouring Who-hit-John down his gullet.

"Back off, mister," came the low-voice warning. "This is none of your business."

"You're right," Fargo said. "I reckon that makes me a damn fool, but so be it. Back off and leave the boy alone."

The man standing farthest back suddenly said, "Kill 'em both!"

Colt flame bloomed in the darkness of the alley. Fargo went to a knee behind a rain barrel. A slug chewed off splinters that stung Fargo's face. The Colt roared and bucked in his hand as he thumbed off several swift shots.

One man yelled in pain; another let out a low groan. Fargo heard a bullet whistle past his head as another slug thumped into the caked mud beside him.

The young man started to stir. His senses were coming back after being knocked out of him by his hard fall. He was lying in the open, too vulnerable to all the lead flying around.

Fargo carried out the border shift, tossing his gun from right hand to left, catching it in midair and firing less than a heartbeat later. At the same time he reached out and grabbed the young man's collar with his right hand.

The muscles of Fargo's arm and shoulders bunched under the buckskin shirt as he hauled the youngster out of the middle of the alley and into the meager protection of the rain barrel. A bullet clipped Fargo's hat while he was doing that and sent it spinning off his head.

With a grunt of effort, Fargo half threw and half rolled the young man against the wall of the building. He had only one shot left in the Colt's cylinder, and it didn't look like there would be time to reload. The man who had been giving the orders barked another command.

"Rush 'em!"

The other men hesitated. Fargo knew he had wounded at least one of them, and clearly they didn't relish the prospect of charging straight toward his gun. He was ready to use that last bullet and then pull the Arkansas Toothpick from the sheath strapped to his calf. He could do a lot of damage with the knife's long, heavy, razor-sharp blade.

It wasn't going to come to that, though, because curious shouts sounded from the mouth of the alley. Townspeople were coming to see what all the shooting was about, and the would-be killers didn't want that many witnesses around.

Fargo heard a muttered curse, and then the leader of the hardcases snapped, "Let's get out of here!"

The command was followed by the thud of rapid

footsteps retreating along the hard-packed dirt of the alley.

Fargo could have sent a shot after them to hurry them along, but he didn't bother. They were already fleeing. He was unhurt, and he hoped the young man he had rescued wasn't seriously injured, either.

"Get a lantern!" a man yelled out on Commerce Street. "Somebody's been murdered back there in the alley!"

Well, that wasn't exactly the case, thought Fargo. The young man moaned and tried to sit up. Fargo quickly reloaded the Colt, then holstered it and took the youngster's arm.

"Are you hit?" he asked as he helped the young man sit up.

"I . . . I don't think so. But I . . . oh, Lord! . . . I'm gonna be sick—"

Fargo stood and stepped back as the young man retched against the wall. The alley didn't smell too good to start with, and the stink got worse.

Flickering light washed over the huddled figure as several men came down the alley, one of them carrying a lantern. Fargo saw that the other men carried shotguns and rifles. They were ready for whatever trouble they might find.

"Take it easy, boys," Fargo told them in a low, powerful voice. "The ruckus is over."

"What happened?" one of the men asked. He was fat, with a walrus mustache hanging down over his mouth. In the lantern light, Fargo saw that he had a star pinned to his vest.

"Three men jumped this fella here," Fargo explained, nodding toward the young man as he spoke. The youngster had stopped throwing up and was trying to push himself to his feet by leaning against the wall of the building. He was still unsteady, but not as drunk as he had been.

"There was a lot of shootin'," the local lawman said. "Either of you need a sawbones?"

Fargo shook his head. "I don't. I'm pretty sure he wasn't hit, either."

The youngster had made it to his feet. He leaned against the wall and shook his head. His face was covered with sweat, and he was pale as milk.

"I'm all right," he managed to say. "Just . . . just feel a mite poorly."

The lawman snorted. "Hell, you look like death warmed over, son. What you need is a pot o' good strong black coffee."

The young man moaned and hunched over, but there was nothing left in his stomach to come up.

"Don't I know you?" the lawman went on. "You're the Forrestal boy, aren't you?"

The youngster nodded shakily. "Yeah. Vance Forrestal."

Fargo had never heard of him before, but evidently the name was known in Fort Worth.

The lawman swung toward Fargo. "Who are you, mister, and what's your part in this?"

Fargo answered the second question first. "I saw this young fella in the Top Notch Saloon tossing back the whiskey, and I had a hunch he might wind up in trouble. My name's Skye Fargo."

"Huh," the badge-toter said. "I know that name. You're the one they call the Trailsman."

Fargo nodded. "That they do, sometimes."

"How'd you know somebody was after young Forrestal here?"

"I saw some men in the saloon watching him. They looked like hardcases, and I could tell by the way they acted they were thinking about robbing him."

"Wasn't . . . wasn't what they were after," Forrestal said fuzzily. "They wanted me *dead*."

That was the way it had seemed to Fargo, too,

9

during the heat of battle in the alley. He knew his first impression in the saloon had been wrong. And he was curious why the three men had wanted to kill Vance Forrestal.

But he was curious about a few other things, too, and he wanted answers to those questions before he made up his mind about what was going on here.

"If you don't need me anymore, Sheriff . . ."

"Hold on there," the lawman said sharply as Fargo started toward the mouth of the alley. "I ain't done with you, Fargo. And I'm the town marshal, not the sheriff. Bert Hinchcliffe's the name."

"Sorry, Marshal," Fargo said. "I always try to cooperate with the law."

But the delay was chafing at him, and he wanted to get back to the saloon. He had a hunch at least some of the answers he wanted were waiting for him there.

"You said you saw three hardcases in the saloon," Hinchcliffe went on. "Are you sure it was the same fellas you swapped lead with out here in the alley?"

"I'm convinced it was, but I couldn't swear to it in court," Fargo said. "It was too dark to get a good look at them."

"What did they look like? The ones in the Top Notch, I mean."

Quickly, Fargo described the three men as best he could, although there hadn't been that much to distinguish them. They were just the sort of hard-faced, beard-stubbled, roughly dressed men who could be found drifting across the West almost anywhere.

Marshal Hinchcliffe turned to Vance Forrestal. "What about you? Did you recognize anybody while you was drinkin'?"

Forrestal shook his head and grimaced at the

pain the movement caused him. "No, but you've got to remember, Marshal, I was pretty drunk."

"You ain't quite sober yet, I'd wager," Hinchcliffe said dryly.

The young man hiccupped. "N-no, Marshal, I'm not. But I'm getting there."

"How come you said those hombres wanted to kill you, instead of just robbin' you?"

Forrestal frowned. "Did I say that? I must have been mistaken. I'm sure they were just . . . just ordinary robbers and c-cutthroats."

Now that was a mite interesting, thought Fargo. Vance Forrestal was changing his story. A few minutes ago, the three hardcases had been assassins. Now they were merely thieves.

Why had Forrestal taken back his accusation?

Fargo didn't know, but again, he thought he might find the answer, or at least a clue, in the saloon. He said impatiently, "Look, Marshal, there's nothing else I can tell you."

"Yeah, all right." Hinchcliffe waved a hand. "You can go, Fargo. You plan to be around Fort Worth for a while?"

"At least tonight. After that I don't know," Fargo answered honestly.

"Reckon I can't hold you to any more than that."

Before leaving the alley, Fargo put a hand on Vance Forrestal's shoulder and asked, "You sure you're all right?"

The young man nodded. "Yeah. Thanks, Mister . . . Fargo, was it?"

"*De nada*. Better watch that boozing in the future."

"Yeah." Forrestal nodded glumly. "You're sure right about that."

Fargo walked out of the alley before the marshal could think of some reason to stop him. He went

11

quickly back to the saloon. Several of the patrons asked him what had happened outside, but he ignored them as he went over to the bar.

The man standing behind the hardwood regarded him nervously. "Something I can do you for, mister?" the bartender asked.

"Roxanne still upstairs?" Fargo asked. He had already looked around the room and confirmed that the dark-haired beauty was nowhere in sight.

The bartender shrugged. "I don't know. I don't keep up with those soiled doves, mister."

Fargo started to nod, but then his hand shot out and bunched up the bartender's dirty apron. He jerked the man forward, pulling him halfway onto the bar. The bartender yelled a curse and flailed, trying to reach under the bar.

Fargo figured the man was trying to get his hands on a bungstarter or some other weapon. Stooping slightly, the Trailsman grasped the wooden grips of the Arkansas Toothpick and slid the big knife out of its sheath. He pressed the tip of the blade against the bartender's throat, just hard enough to make his point without breaking the skin.

"Now," Fargo said, "I'll ask you again. Is Roxanne still upstairs?"

"I . . . I don't know! Be careful with that knife, mister! Ohhhh . . ."

"Let me worry about the knife," Fargo advised. "You just worry about telling me the truth."

The saloon had gone quiet as Fargo held the knife to the bartender's throat. From the corner of his eye Fargo saw a couple of men edging around, trying to get behind him. Probably bouncers, he thought.

"Better tell your boys to stay back," Fargo warned the bartender. "If anybody was to jump me, I might just shove this Toothpick clean through your neck before I knew what was going on."

He wasn't going to do that, of course. But the

bartender didn't know it was a bluff. He choked out, "Stay back! Do what he says!"

"Last time," Fargo intoned ominously. "Roxanne?"

"I don't know!" the bartender said. "I told her to get out of here when she came down after you left! She went back upstairs, and that's the last I seen of her!"

"You were the one who sicced her on me in the first place, right?"

"I . . . I told her to see if she could get you upstairs!"

"Because you noticed me watching that young fella and the three men who were keeping an eye on him. You were in on it with them, weren't you?"

That accusation was partially guesswork on Fargo's part, but he was confident that he was right.

"I . . . I don't know anything about what happened outside! I just knew they didn't want anybody interfering with them."

"They paid you off to see that Forrestal left here drunk as a skunk?"

The bartender tried to shake his head but flinched away from the point of the blade as he did so. Fargo pressed it home inexorably.

"They didn't have to pay me for that! The kid's a boozer, everybody knows that! But they slipped me a few bucks to see that nobody mixed in. I . . . I saw the way you were watchin' them, and I recognized you as Skye Fargo. I know your reputation, mister."

"Where do you know me from?" Fargo asked.

"I saw you a couple of years ago . . . up in Missouri . . . you killed three men in a stand-up gunfight . . . Please, Fargo, don't kill me!"

Fargo leaned closer to him. "One more question. Forrestal was sleeping it off when I went upstairs. Why did he wake up and leave?"

"They . . . they took him out of here! Acted like they were his friends, they did. Said they'd go dunk him in the horse trough and sober him up."

"You knew damn well that wasn't what they had in mind," Fargo grated. "You let them take him out of here to his death."

"Th-the kid's dead?"

"No, but it's no thanks to you that he's not." Fargo gave the man a hard shove that sent him sliding off the bar and stumbling back into a row of shelves lined with liquor bottles. Several tipped over from the impact and shattered on the floor.

"I swear, Fargo, I didn't know what they were going to do! I don't want any trouble in here."

"Too late for that," Fargo growled.

He swung away from the bar and sheathed the Arkansas Toothpick. The crowd parted as he made his way toward the stairs. He didn't expect to find Roxanne, but he was going to check the room where she had taken him.

He was only halfway there when he heard yells and scrambling behind him. Twisting around, he saw that the bartender had pulled a sawed-off shotgun from under the bar.

"Pull a knife on me, will you, you bastard!" he shouted as he jerked the barrels of the deadly weapon toward Fargo.

2

Fargo had no choice in the matter. People were scrambling to get out of the line of fire, but the charges in that sawed-off greener would spread out so wide they could lay waste to half the room.

The bartender was too mad to think about that. He just wanted to kill the man who had threatened and humiliated him.

Fargo drew and fired the Colt in the blink of an eye, hoping to keep the bartender from pulling the triggers on that scattergun.

The bullet drilled through the bartender's shoulder and flung him backward. His finger clenched on the triggers, but the shotgun's barrels were pointed up. The double load of buckshot went into the ceiling, rather than mowing down some of the Top Notch's customers.

The shotgun slipped from the bartender's fingers and fell with a clatter to the floor. He slumped down, clutching his bleeding shoulder.

Fargo said to the room at large, "Somebody fetch a doctor." Then he strode over to look behind the bar at the wounded man.

The bartender snarled up at him. "You killed me, you son of a bitch!"

"You'll live," Fargo told him. "But thanks for

reminding me—do you know those three men? What are their names?"

"I don't know. . . . Never saw them before in my life . . . Ow, that hurts!"

"Not as much as it could have," Fargo said grimly as he holstered his Colt.

This time no one tried to stop him as he climbed the stairs and walked along the balcony to the room he had shared briefly with Roxanne. The door was open a couple of inches. Resting his right hand on the butt of the revolver, Fargo used his left to push the door open.

No shots came from within, or anything else, either. The room was deserted. No sign of Roxanne, although he thought he could detect just a hint of lilac water.

There was no telling where she had gone. Fargo holstered his Colt and went back down the stairs.

He saw that some of the saloon's customers had picked up the wounded bartender and placed him on the bar, with a blanket under him so he wouldn't bleed on the hardwood. As Fargo reached the bottom of the stairs, a little man with bushy side whiskers and eyebrows bustled into the Top Notch, carrying a black bag.

"Where's th' patient?" he asked in a thick Scots burr.

"Over here, Doc," the bartender called. "I think I'm bleedin' to death."

"No' bloody likely," the doctor said as he went over to the bar, the crowd parting to let him through. "I always said yer mangy disposition would get ye shot, Bullock. I'm glad t' see events ha' finally proven me right."

"You're glad I got shot?" the bartender exclaimed, outraged by the very idea.

"Long as 'tis no' fatal. Ye still owe me money, after all. Who ventilated ye?"

The bartender lifted a shaky finger and pointed at Fargo. "There's the man!"

The doctor turned and looked at Fargo, and after a moment he nodded. " 'Twas nice shootin', lad. Ye did no' even break the bone. Friend Bullock here should recover nicely."

Fargo said dryly, "He didn't mention that he was throwing down on me with a greener at the time."

The physician's bushy eyebrows lifted. "Nay, he dinna say anything about that." He extended a hand. "Angus McReady, sir."

"Skye Fargo," the Trailsman introduced himself.

"Doc!" Bullock howled. "You're shakin' hands with the man who shot me, and I'm still bleedin'."

"I'm gettin' there, I'm gettin' there," McReady muttered. He set his bag on the bar, opened it, and began tending to the wounded bartender.

Marshal Bert Hinchcliffe pushed through the bat-wings, started toward the bar, and then stopped short at the sight of Fargo.

"Reckon I should've known," he said, as much to himself as to anyone else. He came on to join the little group beside the bar. "What happened here?"

Bullock said indignantly, "I want to swear out a complaint, Marshal! This fella Fargo came into the saloon and attacked me. He put a knife to my throat!"

Hinchcliffe looked at Fargo. "Any truth to that?"

"It's all true . . . as far as it goes," Fargo said. "I put that knife to Bullock's throat to make him talk. I wanted to know what his connection was with those three hardcases who tried to kill Vance Forrestal."

Hinchcliffe frowned and looked over at Bullock. "You were part o' that?" he asked in a voice rumbling with disapproval.

"I didn't know they were gonna try to kill him!"

Bullock said, desperation edging into his voice. "I didn't know what it was all about. Those men just said they didn't want anybody mixin' in with their plans. For all I knew, it was just some sort of joke!"

Dr. McReady said, "To quote the Bard, methinks thou dost protest too much, Bullock."

"Yeah, what the doc said," Hinchcliffe growled. "You had to know those varmints were up to no good."

"I tell you—" Bullock stopped short in his impassioned defense and let out a howl of pain as the doctor picked up a nearby bottle from the bar and poured whiskey into the shoulder wound. "That's my own whiskey you're killin' me with!" he grated when he could talk again.

"So? I wasna plannin' on chargin' ye for it."

Fargo grinned, feeling an instinctive liking for the feisty little Scots medico. He turned to Hinchcliffe and said, "Do whatever you want about Bullock trying to help those men, Marshal. Do you have a problem with me defending myself from him?"

"Not if he tried to blast you with a shotgun first." Hinchcliffe looked around at the bystanders, several of whom nodded to confirm Fargo's story. The lawman shrugged and went on, "You're in the clear as far as I'm concerned, Fargo. But I'd appreciate it if you'd stop shootin' off guns in my town, at least for the rest of the night."

"I'm a peaceable man, Marshal," Fargo assured him, "as long as everybody else is peaceable, too."

Hinchcliffe just grunted at that.

"What happened to young Forrestal?" Fargo continued.

"I took him home, made sure he was safe and sound where nobody else'll try to ambush him, I hope."

Fargo nodded and then drew the marshal off to

18

the side to indulge his curiosity. "Why do you think those hombres wanted him dead?"

"Vance said he reckoned they wanted to rob him."

Fargo shook his head. "He changed his story, Marshal. At first he said they wanted to kill him."

Hinchcliffe rubbed his jaw and nodded slowly. "Yeah, I noticed that. Thought maybe it was just the heat o' the moment talkin' at first. What do you think?"

"It looked like an attempted killing to me."

"I don't know of any reason for anybody to do that. Robbery I could understand. Vance Forrestal comes from a well-to-do family and usually has money on him. I could even see kidnappin' him and holdin' him for ransom. He's pretty much a no-account young fella, but his pa would probably pay to save his life."

Despite his inclination not to meddle in other people's affairs, Fargo felt himself becoming more intrigued by the evening's events.

"What does he do for a living?"

"Vance? Not much. He's supposed to work at his pa's store, but I don't think he's much of a worker, if you know what I mean."

Fargo nodded. He knew what the marshal meant, all right. He had seen other young men who felt that because their families had money, they didn't have to accomplish anything on their own. Layabouts, wastrels, whatever they were called, Fargo didn't have much use for them.

But then, he had always worked for a living and didn't know any other way to be.

"I don't want to tell you how to do your job, but it might be a good idea to have another talk with Vance and see if you can get to the bottom of this."

Hinchcliffe nodded. "Yeah, I expect you're right,

Fargo. In the meantime, remember what I said about not shootin' up the place."

"Trust me, Marshal, all I'm interested in right now is finding a stable for my horse, a hotel for myself, and a place where I can get something to eat."

"Well, I can help you out on all three of those. Munsey's Livery is right down the street, and so is the Gem Hotel. They've got a dinin' room there, so you won't have to go out again."

"Much obliged," Fargo said. "I've been to Fort Worth before, but it's been a while."

"It's a boomin' little town," Hinchcliffe said with a touch of civic pride.

Fargo nodded good night to the lawman and left the Top Notch. Bullock was still stretched out on the bar, groaning and complaining as Dr. McReady bandaged the wound in his shoulder.

Fargo untied the Ovaro's reins from the hitch rail and led the horse down the street to Munsey's Livery. The stable owner let out a whistle of admiration when he saw the big stallion.

"That's a fine-lookin' piece of horseflesh, mister," he said. "Wouldn't be interested in sellin' him, would you?"

Fargo grinned and patted the Ovaro's shoulder. "When you've been through as much together as this old boy and I have, there wouldn't be any way to put a price on him. Of course, you might get a different answer if you were to ask him if he'd like to sell me."

The Ovaro just snorted as if to say that Fargo was crazy.

With the stableman's promise to take good care of the horse, Fargo left the barn and walked back to the Gem Hotel, which he had spotted as he went down the street earlier. It had been his experience that on the frontier, places named the Gem often weren't very jewel-like. This hotel looked clean, respectable, and comfortable, though.

He had left his saddle at the livery stable, but he was carrying his saddlebags and his Henry rifle as he entered the hotel lobby. The clerk behind the desk didn't seem taken aback by the sight of a man toting a fifteen-shot repeater. It would have been more unusual to see an unarmed man in Fort Worth.

Fargo signed the register and was given the key to room seven. "That's upstairs in the front," the clerk told him. "Got a good view of the street."

"Thanks," Fargo said. "Peaceful town, is it?"

"Oh, yes. There hasn't been a killing in, let's see, three days now. Or is it four? Of course, there was some shooting earlier tonight, but from what I've heard, it didn't amount to much."

Fargo didn't mention that he had been in the middle of that gunplay. He just nodded and went up the stairs to his room. He left his saddlebags on the bed and leaned the Henry in a corner, then returned downstairs and strolled into the hotel's dining room.

A waiter informed him that all the kitchen had left was a pot of beef stew. "Bring it on," Fargo said.

"A bowl of stew, you mean?"

"Unless you want to bring out the whole pot," Fargo replied with a smile. "I've been on the trail for a while, living on jerky and biscuits and beans."

"Well . . . I'll see if I can find a *big* bowl," the waiter compromised.

The stew was good, for Fargo was famished. He ate heartily, and by the time he was finished he wasn't in much of a mood to go back out. He didn't figure he would be too welcome in the Top Notch, and he didn't want to take the trouble to find someplace else to drink and gamble.

Turning in early sounded pretty appealing, he decided.

He climbed the stairs to the second-floor hallway, which was dimly lit by a lamp at each end. His key was in his hand as he approached the door . . . his *left* hand, because his right habitually hovered near the butt of the holstered Colt.

Fargo was about to put the key in the lock when he heard a faint creak on the other side of the door. Instantly he stiffened.

His first thought was that a thief had gotten in there somehow, but hard on the heels of that, he wondered if the intruder could have some connection to what had happened earlier in the night.

Maybe those three hardcases, angry that he had cheated them out of their chosen prey, had tracked him down and were lurking in there in hopes of evening the score.

The intruder might also be one of Bullock's friends seeking revenge for what had happened to the bartender. Fargo didn't figure that Bullock himself would be up to such a thing, the shape he was in.

Regardless of who it was, nobody was supposed to be in there, and Fargo was fairly confident that it wasn't just a friendly visit.

He backed away from the door, moving with a silent grace unusual for a big man. He recalled a narrow balcony, more of a ledge than anything else, that ran along the front of the hotel. Fargo went downstairs and out the front door.

He counted from the corner of the building and found the window to his room. It was dark. The intruder hadn't lit the lamp. The fact that the mysterious visitor was waiting in the dark was further indication that he was up to no good.

Fargo looked around. The hour was late enough so that not many people were on the street, and none were close to the hotel. Satisfied that no one was paying any attention to his actions, he went over to one of the posts supporting that narrow balcony and began to shinny up it.

Being able to climb a tree was an important skill to possess on the frontier. A fella never knew when he might need to escape a rampaging grizzly bear or climb high enough to spot pursuit from Indians. Years of practice and Fargo's natural athletic ability made it easy for him to climb even a fairly smooth pole like this one.

He reached up and caught hold of the railing around the balcony. After that it took him only seconds to swing up and over. The balcony was barely eighteen inches wide, more for decorative purposes than anything else. Fargo moved along carefully toward the window of his room.

Stopping just inches away, he listened intently but didn't hear any noise from inside. It was a warm night. The window was up a couple of inches and the curtains were pulled back to let in fresh air. Fargo knelt beside the window, took his hat off, and risked a look.

His eyes were keen enough so that they didn't need much light. Enough of a glow from the moon and stars fell through the window into the room so that Fargo could make out a dim shape near the door.

Waiting to ambush him, he thought. He grasped the bottom of the window and tested it. It seemed to have been oiled recently, because it slid easily in its tracks and made only a whisper of sound.

Fargo didn't hesitate. He suddenly thrust the window all the way up and went through it in a dive, at the same time flicking his hat toward the intruder. The hat wouldn't do any damage, but it might disorient the man, coming at him out of the darkness like that.

Landing agilely on one knee, Fargo whipped his Colt out and leveled it. "Don't move!" he snapped.

"Oh, my God!" a woman gasped. "Don't shoot! Please don't shoot!"

The voice was familiar to Fargo, though he certainly hadn't expected to hear it in his hotel room. The last place he'd heard it had been in that upstairs room in the Top Notch.

"Roxanne!" he exclaimed as he came to his feet. He didn't holster the Colt. Her presence here could still mean trouble. "What in blazes are you doing?"

"I . . . I wanted to see you again." She came a step closer to him. "I heard about what happened with Vance Forrestal, and I didn't want you to think that I was part of it."

"But you *were* mixed up in it," Fargo said bluntly. "You were supposed to decoy me upstairs so I couldn't interfere."

"I didn't know what was going on, I tell you! Bullock told me to take you upstairs. That's all I knew. He's my boss, so I had to do it."

"He told you my name, too," Fargo said.

"Well, yes, he said you were called Skye Fargo, but—" She stopped short, and in the dim light he saw her raise a hand to her mouth in realization. "When we were together, I called you Skye."

Fargo nodded. "That's right. I hadn't told you my name, so I knew somebody else must have. That's what tipped me off. It didn't have to mean that something was wrong, but it was enough to make me suspicious."

"And when you dumped me on the bed and went out and saw that Vance was gone . . ."

"It was a guess," Fargo said, "but it all fit together."

She rubbed her rump. "I'm glad you threw me on the bed, at least, and not on the floor. It hurt bad enough landing so hard on that thin mattress.

24

And I sure was disappointed when you rushed out of there like that."

"I'm sure," Fargo said dryly.

"No, I mean it!" she insisted. "Bullock may have told me to play up to you, but I promise you, Skye, I wanted to. That's the truth."

Fargo didn't argue with her. He lit a lucifer and held the flame to the wick of the lamp on the little table beside the bed. As the yellow glow filled the room, he saw that Roxanne wore the same low-cut dress she'd had on earlier in the evening.

He pulled the curtains over the window but left the glass up. The drapes danced slightly in the breeze.

"How did you know where to find me?" he asked.

"When I went downstairs, Bullock told me to leave. I guess he was already worried that something was wrong because of the way you'd rushed out. I went up to the room to get a few things, then left by the saloon's back door. From there I circled around and hid in the doorway of a building across the street to sort of keep an eye on the place."

"Why would you do that?"

"Because I wanted to make sure you were all right," she said. "When I saw that you were, I decided that I ought to talk to you and let you know that I didn't mean any harm by what I did. I followed you here to the hotel."

"How'd you know which room I was in?"

She smiled. "It wasn't hard to get a look at the register while the clerk was flirting with me. And it certainly wasn't hard to pick the lock on that door."

Fargo grunted. "You're a woman of many talents."

Roxanne's smile widened. "And I'd be glad to

demonstrate some more of them now, Skye . . . if you'll promise not to throw me on my rump again."

Fargo didn't know what to make of her. She seemed genuine enough in her story, but he still suspected some kind of trick.

She must have sensed his hesitation. "I guess if you don't believe me, I'll just have to prove myself to you."

With that, she reached down and grasped the hem of her dress. Instead of getting him to unfasten the buttons that ran down the back of the garment, she pulled it up and over her head.

She still wasn't wearing anything under it but stockings. She tossed the dress onto the bed and stood before him, letting him appreciate her near nudity.

Cupping her breasts as if offering them to him, she stepped closer.

"What do you say, Skye? Do you want me?"

He wanted her, all right. He felt an ache deep in his gut from wanting her so bad. But he was still cautious.

"You can see for yourself that I'm not armed," she said, a faintly mocking edge in her voice.

"I don't know that I'd go so far as to say that," Fargo drawled. "I'd say you're packing some pretty dangerous weapons there."

She was only inches away from him now. He could feel the heat coming off her.

She reached down, stroked the bulge in his buckskin trousers, and whispered, "I could say the same thing for you."

The hell with it, Fargo decided. He would be alert and careful, of course—that was second nature to him—but he didn't think this young woman meant him any harm.

There was only so much temptation that any man

could stand. Despite his reputation, Skye Fargo was only human.

He put his arms around Roxanne and kissed her.

She returned the kiss with a heated enthusiasm that only increased his excitement. He explored her body with his hands while she began taking off his clothes.

They had to break the kiss while she helped him peel off his boots. Then she pulled his trousers off. She pushed him down into a sitting position on the edge of the bed and knelt in front of him, bringing his stiffly erect member even with her face.

She wrapped her hands around the long, thick pole of male flesh and leaned closer to it. Her eyes were big with excitement and admiration. She rubbed her chin and cheeks over the head of his shaft and then planted a kiss on the tip of it, making a little sound of satisfaction as it throbbed in her hands.

"Just take it easy and enjoy this, Skye," she said huskily. She opened her mouth and enveloped his manhood, running her tongue around the crown before she closed her lips and began to suck gently.

Fargo took a deep breath and closed his eyes for a moment as waves of sheer pleasure went through him. He didn't keep his eyes closed for long—he was too careful for that. No matter how aroused he became, a part of his brain would remain alert.

He had to admit that Roxanne was mighty good at what she was doing. One hand steadied his shaft as she took more and more into her mouth, while the other cupped the heavy sacs at the base and rolled them gently from side to side. When she squeezed them lightly, Fargo thought for a second that he was going to climax then and there, but she pulled back with expert timing and let his arousal subside slightly.

"I can keep going all night," she said proudly.

"Maybe you can," Fargo told her, "but I reckon that'd kill me."

She ran her hands up and down the length of his shaft.

"Come to think of it, that might be too much for me, too." A mischievous grin appeared on her face. "We could try, though."

Fargo slipped his hands under her arms, pulling her onto the bed. As he lay back, she stretched out on top of him, their nude bodies molded together.

"Let's try this instead," Fargo suggested. He cupped a hand behind her head and brought her mouth to his again.

Their tongues met and fenced with each other as they kissed. Fargo kneaded the cheeks of her bottom. His rock-hard shaft stuck up between her soft thighs. She closed them around it and rubbed back and forth in a maddening motion.

He felt the pace of her breathing increase. Roxanne was becoming quite excited, too. She finally lifted her mouth from his and gasped, "I need you inside me, Skye!"

Fargo needed to be inside her, too. He steadied her as she spread her legs and straddled his hips. Pushing herself up, she poised above his shaft and gripped it with her hand, guiding the head to the wet cleft of her sex. She sank down slowly, taking him in inch by inch.

Fargo fought the urge to thrust upward with his hips and bury his full length inside her. Instead, he allowed her to engulf him at her own pace. After what seemed like forever, he was all the way in, with her buttocks resting on his thighs.

"Oh, my Lord!" she exclaimed. "I . . . I don't think I've ever been this full." She seemed dizzy and disoriented for a second, but then she focused on Fargo again and added, "That's not just whore talk, Skye. I . . . I never really felt anything like this before.''

Fargo flexed his hips and moved inside her. If he had his way, she would feel a lot of things before this night was over.

Roxanne cried out softly and met his thrust with one of her own. They started slowly, moving in the timeless rhythm of a man and a woman coming together as one. Fargo's arousal grew even stronger, although he would have said that was probably impossible. He found out that it wasn't.

He reached up and caressed her breasts as she braced her hands on his broad, muscular chest. She rode him like he was a fine stallion, galloping strongly toward a destination they both wanted to reach.

Fargo knew that it wouldn't take them long to scale the heights of passion. As Roxanne's hips began to pump harder, he moved his hands from her breasts to her hips to steady her again. She cried out as her fingernails dug into the flesh of his chest.

Fargo thrust harder in and out, withdrawing and then surging back fully inside her. As his climax boiled up his shaft, he drove into her again and then held himself there at the point of greatest penetration. His seed exploded in white-hot spurts and mixed with the juices flooding from her. Roxanne gasped and shuddered as her culmination rippled through her.

Both of them were drenched.

With a long, low moan, she collapsed on his chest as the last of her spasms faded away. Fargo's shaft throbbed a final time as Roxanne's inner muscles clutched it.

The two of them were breathless and covered with a fine sheen of sweat. The breeze that fluttered the curtains over the window felt mighty good right about now, Fargo thought. His eyes strayed in that direction.

The curtains fluttered again, a little too much this time.

Fargo clamped an arm tightly around Roxanne as instinct galvanized his muscles. He rolled swiftly toward the edge of the bed, taking her with him. His other hand shot out and closed around the butt of the Colt where it protruded from the holster on the bedside table.

As Roxanne yelped in alarm and they tumbled off the bed with their arms still around each other, shots blasted from the window and heavy slugs tore through the mattress.

3

They landed with Fargo on the bottom, so that he had to roll again, onto his side, to free his gun arm and get a shot of his own off. He aimed at the flaring spurts of muzzle flame and triggered the Colt.

A man howled in pain. Fargo fired again. This time there was a crash and a scream that lasted only a couple of seconds before it was cut off by a heavy thud.

Fargo heard all that only vaguely because his ears were ringing from the thunderous detonations of guns in the small room. He pushed himself up into a crouch and glanced down at Roxanne.

"Are you all right?"

She was wide-eyed with fear and surprise and panic, but he didn't see any blood on her. She babbled something but couldn't give him a coherent answer. Satisfied that she wasn't wounded, he came to his feet and leaned over to blow out the lamp.

Then he padded quickly to the window and shoved the curtains back with a sweep of his arm. He looked out and saw that the railing along that narrow balcony was broken right in front of the window.

That came as no surprise. He had figured that his bullets had knocked the would-be killer backward through the railing and off the balcony. He resisted the temptation to stick his head out the window and look down into the street to see what had happened to the man.

It was entirely possible that the bushwhacker had partners, and rifles could be trained on the window right now, just waiting for him to poke his head out.

"Get dressed," Fargo snapped. He stepped over to the table and set the gun down for a moment, just long enough to pull his trousers on. Then he picked up the Colt again.

Roxanne climbed shakily to her feet. "Skye," she managed to say after a moment. "Are you hurt?"

"I'm fine," he said. "How about you?"

She had regained her wits, at least to a certain extent. "I'm all right. None of those shots hit me. Wh-what happened?"

"Somebody tried to kill us. Tried to kill me, rather. I don't reckon they were after you. You were just in the way."

"But why?"

"We'll find out once we see who he was."

"You don't think I had anything to do with this? . . ."

Fargo shook his head, then realized she probably couldn't see him in the darkened room. "No, I don't. But I'd be willing to bet the gunman was one of those three hardcases from the Top Notch, the ones who tried to kill Vance Forrestal."

"My God, what's going on here?"

"I intend to find out," Fargo said grimly. He told her again, "Better get dressed. I expect the marshal will be here in a few minutes."

And remembering how Hinchcliffe had asked him to quit shooting up the town, Fargo figured the local lawman wouldn't be very happy, either.

Fargo and Roxanne were both dressed by the time Marshal Bert Hinchcliffe arrived. By then there was a small crowd in the second-floor hallway outside the door of Fargo's room. The hotel clerk and several of the guests had shown up to see what all the shooting was about. Fargo had considered the idea of letting Roxanne slip away before the law arrived, but he couldn't very well do that with so many witnesses around.

Fargo ignored the questions from the curious bystanders, preferring to tell the story only once. When Hinchcliffe tromped up the stairs and reached the second-floor landing, he stopped short at the sight of Fargo standing just outside the open door of the room.

"Tarnation, I should've knowed it," Hinchcliffe muttered. "Fargo, how many shootin' scrapes are you gonna get mixed up in before this night is over?"

"No more, I hope," Fargo replied honestly. "Did you find a body in the street outside?"

Hinchcliffe gave a grim nod.

"I sure did. Fella had two bullet holes in him, either o' which would've done for him, accordin' to Doc McReady. I reckon you're the one who put those holes in him?"

"Check the mattress of the bed in my room," Fargo suggested. "It's all shot up, and that happened before I ever returned fire."

"Ambushed you from the window, did he?" Hinchcliffe looked at Roxanne. "While you were sleepin'?"

"Something like that," Fargo replied.

"None o' my business what you were doin'," Hinchcliffe said with a shrug. "But it might help if you had a witness who could verify that the other fella shot first."

"He did, Marshal," Roxanne said, speaking up without hesitation. "I can testify to that."

Hinchcliffe grunted, as if the word of a soiled

dove didn't mean all that much. He didn't press the matter, however. Instead he asked, "You work at the Top Notch, don't you?"

"That's right."

Hinchcliffe looked at Fargo.

"Does this have anything to do with those other shootin's?"

"I'll have to take a look at the man I killed," Fargo said. "I'd be willing to bet, though, that he's one of the three who went after Vance Forrestal."

"I got a hunch you're right." Hinchcliffe jerked his head toward the stairs. "Come on. The carcass is over at Shannon's place. He's the local undertaker."

Fargo put a hand briefly on Roxanne's shoulder and squeezed. "I'll see you later," he told her. He was confident that she wouldn't be in any danger as long as she wasn't around him. He'd been the bushwhacker's target, not her.

Fargo and Hinchcliffe went downstairs and left the hotel. Hinchcliffe led the way to the local undertaking parlor. They met Dr. Angus McReady emerging from the establishment.

"What's the verdict, Doc?" Hinchcliffe asked. "The fella still dead?"

"Dead as can be," McReady replied. He looked at Fargo. "Well, well. My guess would be that you're the one responsible for that fellow's, ah, grave condition."

"Seemed like the thing to do at the time," Fargo said, "considering that he was trying his damnedest to kill me."

Hinchcliffe started for the door. "Let's go take a look at him."

McReady followed, evidently out of curiosity. Hinchcliffe greeted the undertaker, a red-haired, florid-faced Irishman, who ushered them into a room where the air held the unpleasant tang of chemicals. The dead man, naked now, was stretched out on a table.

Fargo's jaw tightened. He wasn't going to lose any sleep over killing this gunman; as he'd said, the man had been trying to kill him. But seeing him laid out like that was rather grotesque and disconcerting.

He had studied the faces of the three men in the Top Notch Saloon as they were watching Vance Forrestal, and it took only a glance for Fargo to confirm his guess. The dead bushwhacker was a member of that hardcase trio.

With a nod, Fargo said to Hinchcliffe, "He's one of them, all right. If there was any doubt about who I traded shots with in that alley, this ought to end it."

"I reckon," Hinchcliffe agreed. "You kept 'em from grabbin' young Forrestal—or killin' him, if that's what they were really tryin' to do—and they were mad enough about it to come after you later."

Fargo nodded again. "That's the way I see it, too, Marshal."

Hinchcliffe frowned and pulled at his walrus mustache.

"What worries me about that is . . . them other two are still out there somewhere."

"I promise you, I've already thought of that," Fargo said with a humorless smile.

"What're you gonna do about it?"

"What can I do about it?" Fargo asked with a shrug. "I don't know who they are, where they've gone, or what they wanted with Forrestal. All I can do is hope they don't ambush me again—and be ready if they do."

Marshal Hinchcliffe wasn't too happy about letting Fargo return to the hotel, but since Fargo hadn't really broken any laws the marshal couldn't just lock him up . . . although Hinchcliffe did allow that things might quiet down if he did it anyway.

Fargo was watchful for any signs of trouble or impending danger as he walked back to the Gem. When he reached the hotel, he saw that the crowds had dispersed. The lobby was empty except for the clerk behind the desk.

"Mr. Fargo, you're in room eleven now," the clerk called as the Trailsman crossed the lobby. He held up a key.

Fargo walked over to the desk and took the key.

"How come you moved me?" he asked.

"Well . . . somebody tried to kill you in room seven." The clerk looked and sounded like it should have been obvious why Fargo wouldn't want to stay there.

"If I avoided every place somebody's tried to kill me, there wouldn't be many places west of the Mississippi where I could stay," Fargo said.

"Maybe so, but the mattress is shot full of holes, and it'll take a while to get a new one. Don't worry, nobody messed with your saddlebags or your rifle. I carried 'em down to the new room myself."

"All right," Fargo said. "Room eleven it is. I'm obliged, I guess."

"It's a better room anyway," the clerk said. "It's on the front, like seven, but it's a corner room, so it's a little bigger and has better ventilation."

Fargo nodded and turned toward the stairs, but he paused long enough to say over his shoulder, "If anybody comes looking for me, I don't want to be disturbed. It's been sort of a long evening, and I'm a mite tuckered."

"Of course, Mr. Fargo."

He went up to the new room and let himself in, halfway expecting to find Roxanne waiting there for him. Or one or both of those hard cases who had a grudge against him.

Instead the room was empty, and the bed was inviting. Fargo locked the door, then undressed and stretched out. Like a big cat, he was asleep almost instantly.

His slumber was deep and dreamless, although as always, a small part of his brain remained alert and would rouse him instantly if danger threatened.

When he awoke the next morning, sunlight was already slanting through the gaps in the curtains over the windows.

Fargo stretched the kinks out of his muscles, climbed into his clothes, buckled his gun belt and the holstered Colt around his waist, strapped the sheathed Arkansas Toothpick to his calf. He went downstairs in search of coffee and some breakfast.

The dining room was nearly full. Conversation fell off as Fargo entered. Obviously, word had gotten around about the shootings the night before. Fargo tried not to grimace. He didn't like being the center of attention, especially when it was because he'd had to ventilate a couple of fellas, one of them fatally.

Finding an empty table, he dropped his hat on the floor next to a chair and sat down. This morning there was a waitress on duty, a plump, pretty young woman with blond hair. She came over to Fargo and said, "Good morning, sir. What can I get you?"

"A pot of coffee, black as sin, a stack of flapjacks, hash browns, eggs . . . You have bacon?"

"No, sir, I'm sorry. But we do have ham."

"Two or three thick slices of ham, then," Fargo said with a nod. "Finish it off with some biscuits and molasses."

"Yes, sir." She smiled. "That's quite an order."

Fargo returned the smile.

"I'm just a growing boy," he told her.

"I'll bet that's right, sir," she said with a twinkle

in her eyes, and there was an extra, saucy toss to her hips as she turned toward the kitchen door.

Fargo enjoyed the casual flirting, but that was all it amounted to. Once he was alone at the table, he started thinking about everything that had happened the night before, and his demeanor grew more solemn.

Something strange was going on in Fort Worth. The attack on Vance Forrestal hadn't been a simple robbery attempt. Fargo was certain of that.

It was none of his business why somebody wanted the young man dead, of course, but Fargo was curious anyway. Vance had seemed harmless enough. A little pathetic, maybe, because he was such a drunk at a young age, but that wasn't worth killing him over.

The murmur of conversation in the room had returned to its previous level. Now it died away again, and as Fargo glanced up and saw who had just come into the dining room, he muttered, "Speak of the devil."

Vance Forrestal had paused just inside the open double doors that led from the hotel lobby into the dining room. He was looking around, and when his searching gaze found Fargo, he started across the room toward the table where the Trailsman sat.

Vance's pallid face was haggard and drawn this morning. Clearly he was suffering from the after-effects of his binge the night before. But his voice was fairly steady as he came up to the table, rested a hand on the back of an empty chair, and asked, "You mind if I sit down?"

"Help yourself," Fargo said.

Vance pulled back the chair and settled himself on it. He took off the bowler hat he was wearing and placed it on the table.

"You're Skye Fargo."

The youngster paused as if waiting for a response, so Fargo said, "That's right."

"I asked around about you. You're a well-known guide and scout. People even call you the Trailsman."

"You're not telling me anything I don't already know," Fargo said a little impatiently.

"I'm sorry. I meant to come in and get right down to business, but this head of mine . . ."

He closed his eyes, raised a hand to his forehead, and massaged his temples for a moment. It didn't seem to help much.

The blond waitress approached the table carrying a coffeepot in one hand and a cup and saucer in the other. As she set them down, Fargo asked, "Would you be kind enough to bring another cup, ma'am?"

"Of course." She hurried off to fulfill the request.

"What you need is some black coffee," Fargo told Vance Forrestal.

"It won't do a bit of good." The young man laughed, but there was no humor in the sound. "Believe me, I know. I've tried every cure in existence for this misery."

"Have you tried not drinking if you can't handle it?"

Vance shook his head. "I'm afraid that's not an option."

Fargo's mouth tightened. He liked a drink as much as the next man, but he didn't care for people who let whiskey rule their lives and then acted like it wasn't their fault.

Still, he wasn't the sort to pass judgment on folks as long as they weren't hurting anybody but themselves. If Vance Forrestal wanted to booze his life away, that was his business.

Fargo was still a mite curious about why those three hardcases had been after him, though.

The waitress came back with a second cup. Fargo

poured it full of coffee and told Vance, "Drink that. At least you'll be a little more awake, if nothing else."

The waitress said, "Your food will be here in a minute, Mr. Fargo." She looked at Vance. "Would you like something to eat, Mr. Forrestal?"

Vance had just picked up his cup. He shuddered so hard at the thought of food that some of the coffee nearly sloshed out onto the table.

"No, thanks, Margaret. I'll just stick with coffee."

She nodded and went away, but not before she gave an eloquent sigh of disapproval.

Vance noticed that. He said quietly, "I'm afraid the good citizens of Fort Worth don't think much of me. They consider me a rich young wastrel who has more money than sense."

"From what I've seen, that's just about right," Fargo said.

Vance sipped his coffee and then chuckled, and this time he sounded more genuinely amused.

"I certainly can't argue with that conclusion, based on the evidence," he said. "But I'm not totally hopeless or helpless, Mr. Fargo. Sometimes my whiskey-soaked stupor is interrupted by moments of clarity, such as this one." He paused and then went on, "I want to hire you."

Fargo was a little taken aback by that blunt statement.

"Hire me to do what?" he asked.

"Get me to San Antonio, and keep me alive along the way." Vance took another sip of the steaming coffee. "You see, I'm getting married."

All this was coming at Fargo a little too fast. He was glad that the waitress arrived then with his breakfast, so he had an opportunity to think about what Vance had just said.

Vance shuddered again as Fargo dug into the food and washed it down with sips of the strong

40

black coffee. After a few minutes, Fargo said, "Before I say anything about that job offer, I'll have to know more."

"Ask anything you want," Vance replied as he warmed his hands on the coffee cup. He was still pale, but he didn't seem quite as shaky as he had when he came into the hotel dining room.

"Who were those three men who attacked you last night?"

"I don't know their names. I never saw them before."

Fargo shook his head in disgust.

"If you're not going to play straight with me—"

"I don't know them," Vance insisted, "but I do know who sent them, and why."

That was more like it. Fargo nodded and said, "Go on."

"They were sent to kill me. Hired assassins, I suppose you could call them."

"That's what I figured. That business about them wanting to rob you was a lie."

"Yes, after I blurted out the truth to the marshal, I thought it might be wise to change my story."

"Why?" Fargo snapped.

"There's a need for . . . discretion. After you hear more, I hope you'll understand, Mr. Fargo."

"Keep talking," Fargo said.

"I told you I'm getting married." Vance took a deep breath. "I believe my prospective father-in-law is the one who sent those men to kill me."

Fargo set his knife and fork down but continued slowly chewing the food he had in his mouth. When he had swallowed, he asked, "Why would he want you dead?"

"The obvious reason, of course: he doesn't want me to marry his daughter."

"There are better ways to deal with an unwanted son-in-law than having him killed."

Vance laughed wryly.

"Yes, but none more efficient. A dead groom does away with any chance for a wedding."

"Keep talking."

"Gladly. It's one of the few things I do well."

Over the next few minutes, Vance Forrestal explained that his father was a successful merchant here in Fort Worth, as well as the owner of a freight line that stretched all the way to the Gulf Coast. Isaac Forrestal was a hardheaded, tightfisted businessman who had hoped that his son would follow in his footsteps.

To that end, he had sent Vance on several business trips, ostensibly to look out for his interests but really as more of a test for the young man.

"I failed the test," Vance said easily. It didn't seem to bother him that much. "But I got something out of the trips. When I was in San Antonio last year, I met Sally Pryor."

"The girl you're engaged to," Fargo guessed. He had finished the food but was working on his third cup of coffee.

"That's right. I was in San Antonio for a month, but instead of taking care of the business that brought me there, I spent my time courting Sally. When I had to come back up here to Fort Worth, we continued corresponding, and when I asked her to marry me, she agreed."

"I take it her pa didn't care much for the idea?"

"Her pa doesn't care much for *me*. He certainly didn't like the idea of Sally and me getting married."

"You really think he'd go so far as to hire bushwhackers to kill you?" Fargo asked.

"Have you ever heard of Big Nate Pryor?"

Fargo thought about it and then shook his head. "Can't say as I have."

"He calls himself Nathaniel Pryor now that he's a respectable businessman, but he was Big Nate when he worked on the docks at Indianola, down on the coast."

Fargo nodded. He was familiar with the Gulf Coast port of Indianola. Like all seaport towns, it could be a rough place.

"He bought himself a warehouse there," Vance went on, "and gradually worked his way up to becoming one of the most important men in the region when it comes to shipping goods in and out. He moved to San Antonio, but he still owns warehouses in Galveston, Indianola, and Corpus Christi. My father was hoping to do business with him."

"But you pretty much scotched that, didn't you?" Fargo asked.

"Of course. You've heard of the Midas touch, in Greek mythology?"

Fargo nodded.

"I have just the opposite talent," Vance said. "Everything I touch turns to horse droppings."

"Except for your romance with Sally Pryor."

"Yes, except for that." Vance's self-mocking attitude fell away for a moment as he went on, "Sally's love is the one thing in my life that gives me a bit of hope I might not ruin everything."

"But this Big Nate Pryor plans to put a stop to the wedding before it ever takes place."

"By having me killed, yes," Vance said with a nod.

Fargo leaned back in his chair and drained the last of the coffee in his cup. The crowd in the dining room had thinned out while they were talking, as the other guests went on about their business.

"That's quite a story."

"It's the truth," Vance insisted. "Pryor is ruthless enough to hire gunmen."

"How did you get away from those three last night? The way I hear it, you could barely walk when they took you out of the Top Notch."

"I *couldn't* walk. They pretty much dragged me out, I suppose. But the instinct for self-preservation must have come awake in me when they took me into that alley. Something forced me to come to my senses, at least enough for me to realize that my life was in danger and I'd never get out of there alive unless I did something."

"There was a shot after you started struggling with them," Fargo said. "I heard it."

"They weren't expecting me to fight back. I was able to get my hands on a gun belonging to one of them. I dropped it when I fired that shot, and of course I didn't hit anything, but it distracted them enough so that I was able to pull free. Then I turned and ran."

"And fell flat on your face," Fargo pointed out.

"My legs weren't working too well just then," Vance admitted sheepishly. "But you came along and saved me."

"Damned lucky for you that I did," Fargo said with a grunt.

"You'll get no argument from me on that score, Mr. Fargo. I know that I owe you my life. But there's a Chinese proverb that says once you save someone's life, you're responsible for them from then on."

"I've heard that old saying," Fargo said, "but this is Texas, not China. I just stepped in to lend a hand. As far as I'm concerned, we're square."

"All right. I still want to hire you."

"As a bodyguard," Fargo said flatly.

"Yes, you could call it that. The wedding between myself and Sally is scheduled to take place two weeks from now in San Antonio. That's plenty of time to make the trip by horseback, but I'm afraid I'll be ambushed again along the way."

"Take the stagecoach," Fargo suggested.

Vance shook his head. "Big Nate's gunmen would just stop the stage somewhere along the way, pretend to be holding it up, and then murder me in the course of the so-called robbery."

Fargo had to admit that if Vance was right about the situation, there was a good chance something like that would indeed happen.

"I think I'll be safer riding," Vance went on, "especially if I have you with me, Mr. Fargo. Your reputation might even keep Big Nate's men from coming after us."

"It didn't stop one of those hardcases from trying to kill me last night," Fargo pointed out. "And the other two are probably still lurking around, waiting for their chance."

"All the more reason for us to travel together. Strength in numbers, you know."

Fargo didn't think Vance Forrestal was likely to contribute much strength, but he kept that thought to himself.

Vance went on, "What do you say? I can afford to pay you well. Unless there was somewhere else you have to be . . ."

Fargo shook his head. He wasn't going to lie, even to avoid what looked like it might turn out to be a dangerous, unpleasant business.

"No, I'm just drifting right now."

"Then you can drift to San Antonio with me and make some money in the process."

Fargo didn't particularly like Vance Forrestal. It was obvious, though, that the young man had some powerful, ruthless enemies. There was a good chance Vance *wouldn't* survive to reach San Antonio unless he got some help.

"All right," Fargo said, but not without a certain reluctance. "I'll ride along with you."

He named a fee and added that Vance would also pay for all the supplies and ammunition. The young man nodded eagerly, not even bothering to negotiate.

"Of course. How soon will you be ready to leave?"

"Whenever you are," Fargo said.

"We'll go over to my father's store and get our supplies." Vance sounded excited now. "Maybe we can ride out this afternoon."

"Sure." Fargo regarded his young companion curiously. "I've got just one more question."

"What's that?"

"Say you make it to San Antonio and marry this girl. What happens then? Are you going to spend the rest of your life looking over your shoulder and worrying that your father-in-law is going to have you killed?"

"It won't come to that," Vance replied with conviction. "Once Sally and I are married, Big Nate will see that she's happy, and he'll get used to the idea."

Fargo nodded slowly. Vance might believe that, but Fargo wasn't convinced.

This journey to San Antonio might be just the beginning of the young man's troubles.

4

Vance didn't own a horse, so Fargo went with him to the livery stable to pick out a good mount.

"You *can* ride, can't you?" Fargo asked. "It's a little over three hundred miles to San Antonio. You'll be mighty sore before we get there if you're not used to a saddle."

"I can ride," Vance assured him. "I've ridden for as far back as I can remember. I just don't have a horse of my own. They all belong to my family."

That comment reminded Fargo of something.

"How does your family feel about you getting married? Are they as opposed to the idea as Big Nate Pryor is?"

Vance shrugged and shook his head.

"My parents and my sisters have pretty much given up on me, Mr. Fargo. They think whatever I try to do is doomed. Given my record, they have every reason to think that, of course."

"They're not coming to San Antonio for the wedding?"

"They don't believe there will ever be a wedding. I think they're hoping that Sally will come to her senses and refuse to marry me."

Fargo frowned. His dislike for Vance Forrestal was growing. He wasn't sure he had made the right decision when he agreed to accompany the young man to San Antonio. Listening to Vance's maudlin self-pity for three hundred miles might be more than Fargo could stand.

But a deal was a deal, and he recalled that they had shaken on it before leaving the hotel. So Fargo had no choice but to go ahead and honor his end of the bargain.

Marshal Bert Hinchcliffe was standing in front of the livery stable, talking to the proprietor, when Fargo and Vance walked up.

"I was hopin' I'd run into you this mornin', Fargo," the lawman said. "The inquest into that fella's death is at ten o'clock. I'd be obliged if you were there."

Fargo nodded. "That's all right. I'm leaving town, but not until this afternoon."

"I won't lie to you—I'll be glad to see you ride out. Hell seems to have a habit o' poppin' when you're around, Fargo." Hinchcliffe looked at Vance Forrestal. "What are the two o' you doin' to-gether?"

Vance answered the marshal's question.

"Mr. Fargo and I are going to be traveling to-gether. We're leaving for San Antonio this after-noon."

Hinchcliffe grunted in surprise.

"Is that so? Well, good luck to you, Fargo." He looked at Vance again and shook his head. "You're liable to need it."

After telling Fargo where the inquest would be held, Hinchcliffe went on his way. Fargo told the stable owner that they needed a horse for Vance, and the man led them over to the corral and pointed out several mounts that he had for sale.

They settled on a rangy dun, Vance relying on Fargo to make the final decision.

"That's a smart move, son," the stable keeper told him. "Mr. Fargo here knows horseflesh. If you don't believe me, take a look at the stallion he's ridin'."

The man pointed at the Ovaro, who had emerged from his stall and come out into the corral. Vance let out a whistle of admiration, much as the stable owner had done the night before when Fargo brought in the stallion.

"I'm no expert, but that looks like a fine horse to me."

"He is," Fargo agreed. "That dun we picked out for you isn't bad, either. Now, let's round up those supplies. You could use some better traveling clothes, too."

Vance looked down at his brown tweed suit.

"What's wrong with this outfit?"

"It's not made for riding that far, for one thing. For another, it's going to look damned silly when we're out on the trail."

"Oh. Well, then, I place myself in your hands, Mr. Fargo. Mold me as though I were nothing but common clay."

Lord help us all, Fargo thought.

He left Vance in the Forrestal Emporium while the clerks were filling their order and walked down Main Street to the Tarrant County Courthouse, just short of the bluff overlooking the Trinity River where the army post was located. There was talk that the army might close the fort, but so far it was still garrisoned.

The inquest was over in short order. Fargo testified to what had happened, saying that a young lady had been visiting him in his hotel room without mentioning Roxanne's name or giving any more details, when the deceased opened fire on them from the window. Fargo stated that he had returned the fire and knocked the bushwhacker off the balcony.

Marshal Hinchcliffe confirmed Fargo's story and testified that all the physical evidence he had seen—the broken railing on the balcony and the dead hardcase lying in the street—backed up what Fargo had to say.

The would-be killer had not been identified. He was just one of countless drifters who had been willing to sell his gun and who had died for his trouble.

The six members of the coroner's jury returned a quick verdict of self-defense and then thanked Fargo for his service to the community in ridding it of a bushwhacking varmint. With that, the coroner, who happened to be Dr. Angus McReady, brought his gavel down and dismissed the proceedings.

Outside the courthouse, Fargo paused to talk briefly with Marshal Hinchcliffe and Dr. McReady.

"Fargo here is headin' for San Antone with the Forrestal boy," Hinchcliffe told the doctor.

"Is that so?" McReady responded, raising his bushy eyebrows in surprise.

Hinchcliffe nodded and looked at Fargo.

"I hear tell the two of you even had breakfast together in the dining room at the Gem."

"I had breakfast," Fargo corrected. "Vance was too hungover to be able to stomach anything except some black coffee."

"I don't suppose the young fella had any more to say about why those hardcases jumped him last night?"

Fargo hesitated. He didn't make a habit of lying to the law, but Vance wanted to keep quiet concerning his suspicions about his prospective father-in-law being behind the ambush. He had told Fargo only because he felt that he had to in order to convince the Trailsman to accept his job offer.

Fargo could see why the whole situation was a

little embarrassing to the young man. And telling Hinchcliffe wouldn't serve any real purpose, since they were leaving Fort Worth and no more trouble relating to the situation was likely to happen in the marshal's bailiwick.

"He didn't say anything about it. I reckon maybe it was just a robbery."

"Maybe, but I ain't convinced," Hinchcliffe said. "I'd keep both eyes open whilst ridin' with that boy, if I was you, Fargo."

"I intend to," Fargo said.

When he got back to the emporium and saw the supplies piled on the counter, he told Vance, "We're going to need a pack animal, too. I'll see about that at the stable. Did you get some better riding clothes?"

"Yes, I did, just as you suggested, Mr. Fargo. Or should I call you Skye?"

"Skye will do fine, since we'll be riding together."

Vance grinned.

"I never thought I'd be on a first name basis with a famous frontiersman."

"Well, we're even, because I never figured I'd be riding to San Antonio with somebody like you, either," Fargo told him.

Before Vance could ask him what he meant by that, Fargo went on to say that they would leave around one o'clock and to meet in front of the livery stable.

"I'll see to it that all this gear is taken over there and loaded on the packhorse I pick out," he explained. He looked around the well-stocked, high-ceilinged store. "So this is your father's place. Where is he?"

"Oh, he's not here," Vance said with a shake of his head. "He doesn't actually run the store anymore. He has a manager for that. He'll be at home,

I expect, brooding on what a failure his son turned out to be."

Fargo nodded.

"I'll see you later. One o'clock, remember?"

"I'll be there," Vance promised.

"One more thing," Fargo said. "Do you have a gun?"

"I have a pocket pistol. Why?"

Instead of answering, Fargo caught the eye of one of the clerks and called the man over. Pointing into a glass-topped case, Fargo told the clerk, "We'll need that Colt, and a belt and holster. A Henry rifle, too, if you've got one."

"We sure do, Mr. Fargo." The man glanced nervously at Vance. "Are you and young Mr. Forrestal going hunting?"

"You could say that," Fargo replied dryly.

There might be some hunting involved during the trip to San Antonio, he thought, but likely he and Vance would be the hunted, not the hunters.

He left the store and strolled around Fort Worth for a few minutes, thinking about the upcoming journey to make sure he hadn't overlooked anything. He wasn't paying that much attention to where his steps took him, so he was a little surprised when he looked up and realized he was standing in front of the Top Notch Saloon.

He hadn't meant to come here, but now that he had, maybe it was a good idea, Fargo thought. He could step inside and say good-bye to Roxanne. Even though she had helped distract him when the three hardcases went after Vance, she hadn't known what was going on.

Fargo walked into the saloon. A tall, bald-headed man was working behind the bar. Bullock was nowhere in sight.

Since the hour was not quite noon, the saloon wasn't very busy. Half a dozen men stood at the bar, drinking, and four more sat at a table playing poker. The men at the bar were an even mix of soldiers and townies. One soldier sat in on the card game, too. The dealer was a slick-haired professional gambler.

If any of the saloon's patrons recognized Fargo, they gave no sign of it. The bald-headed apron drifted down the bar toward him and asked, "Want a drink, mister?"

"I reckon it's late enough," Fargo said. "Make it beer, though, instead of whiskey."

"You pays your money, you names your poison," the bartender said with a grin. He bent to draw a mug of beer from a barrel under the bar.

"Has Roxanne been down this morning?" Fargo asked as the man set the beer in front of him.

"Haven't seen her. It's early yet, for any of the girls to be stirring. They don't come downstairs until later in the afternoon, around three or four."

Fargo nodded and took a healthy swallow of the beer.

"Reckon it'd be all right if I went up and knocked on her door?"

"It's all right with me," the bartender replied with a shrug. "Some of those gals, though, they're liable to take a knife to you if you disturb their beauty sleep."

"I'll take my chances."

Carrying his mug of beer, Fargo started for the stairs. He climbed to the second floor and went along the balcony to the door of Roxanne's room. He knocked softly, not wanting to wake any of the other soiled doves.

There was no answer. Fargo knocked a little harder.

Still no reply.

Frowning slightly, Fargo tried the knob. The door was unlocked. He twisted the knob and pushed the door open, stepping inside as he called softly, "Roxanne?"

She wasn't there.

In the light of day coming in through the open window, the room was even smaller, more cramped and squalid than it had seemed the night before. The sheets on the bed were tangled, as if Roxanne had thrashed around in her sleep—or thrashed around on them for some other reason.

Fargo wasn't about to get jealous of a whore, even one he genuinely liked as he did Roxanne. He had no idea why she wasn't in her room at this hour of the day, but although he regretted that he wouldn't get to say good-bye to her, he wasn't going to worry about it.

He started to back out of the room.

But as he reached for the knob to pull the door shut, he froze. Something had caught his eye, and suddenly he took a couple of quick steps forward and bent to study a pair of small, dark stains on the floor. He touched one of the spots with a fingertip.

The substance was almost dry, but still just a little sticky. Fargo saw a few more spots. They led toward the open window. He rubbed his fingers together thoughtfully.

Those stains came from drops of blood landing on the floor. There was no doubt of that in his mind. And to his keen, experienced eyes, they formed a trail leading from the side of the bed directly to the window.

Fargo moved to the window. The glass was up all the way. Nothing unusual about that. It had been a warm night, and Roxanne could have opened it to get all the fresh air she could.

He studied the sill, leaning out the window a little to do so. Again he saw something unusual. There were twin spots on the sill, a little more than a foot apart, where the dust had been disturbed and something had rubbed on the wood.

A ladder would leave marks like that, Fargo thought, if somebody propped it in the window and climbed up from the alley below.

Despite the warmth of the day, Fargo felt an icy finger trace a path along his spine. If he hadn't noticed those little bloodstains on the floor, he would have turned around and left Fort Worth without ever having any notion that something was wrong.

Now he was certain that during the night someone had climbed through that window and taken Roxanne out of here by force.

But who, and why, and where had she been taken?

And maybe most important of all, had those drops of blood come from her abductor . . . or from her?

Was she even still alive?

Fargo wheeled around and stalked out of the room in a hurry, leaving the half-empty mug of beer on the small table next to Roxanne's rumpled bed. He wasn't thirsty anymore.

Downstairs, he went straight to the bar. The bald-headed bartender came over and raised his eyebrows quizzically.

"Something else you need, mister?"

Fargo jerked his head toward the balcony.

"You hear any sort of ruckus in those upstairs rooms?"

"No, but I just came on duty at eight this morning. By then, none of the gals had customers anymore and they were all asleep."

So the abduction had probably taken place before then, Fargo thought. In the early morning hours, anybody still in the saloon was likely to be so drunk that they wouldn't have heard anything, even if Roxanne had raised a commotion. And it was possible that the kidnapping had been carried out so quietly that no one would have heard it downstairs anyway.

"Something wrong?" the bartender asked with a frown.

Fargo considered for a second and then shook his head. Nobody was going to get too worked up over a whore being abducted . . . nobody but him.

And there was something else to think about. After everything that had happened the night before, Fargo thought it was possible Roxanne's disappearance might be connected to Vance Forrestal's trouble. The men who were after Vance knew that Fargo and Roxanne had been together last night. Maybe they had grabbed her to use as leverage.

If that was the case, then going to the law might put Roxanne in even more danger than she already was. On the other hand, maybe they had grabbed her just as a matter of revenge, thinking that Fargo might be fond of her. It worked either way.

And either way, Fargo couldn't do much about it except wait to see what the next play in this game would be.

He didn't have long to wait. As he pushed the batwings aside and stepped out of the saloon, a shambling, disheveled figure ran into him. Fargo stepped back and put his hand on the butt of his Colt, but he didn't draw it when he saw that the man who had collided with him was a ragged old-timer.

"Sorry, mister," the old man muttered. Rheumy eyes narrowed as he studied Fargo. "Say, you're the one they call the Trailsman, ain't you?"

"That's right," Fargo replied with a curt nod.

The old-timer reached into the pocket of his stained, tattered coat.

"I got somethin' for you."

Fargo watched him closely, just in case a gun came out of that pocket. Instead, the old man brought forth a folded piece of paper. He held it out to Fargo.

"Where did you get that?" Fargo asked before he took the paper.

"Fella paid me four bits to find you and give it to you. Told me what you looked like an' ever'thing. Seemed mighty generous to me, but I took it. Damn tootin', I did."

Fargo plucked the paper from the old-timer's gnarled fingers and unfolded it. His already grim expression grew even bleaker as he scanned the words crudely printed on it.

BRING VANCE FORRESTAL OR WE KILL THE GIRL. BIG
TREES TEN MILES SOUTH OF TOWN.

Well, that was plain enough, Fargo thought. Vance's life for Roxanne's.

But how could the kidnappers know that he would value Roxanne's life enough to make such a bargain? The answer was simple: they couldn't. They had considered it worth a try; that was all. If Fargo ignored the message, they hadn't really lost anything. They could just kill Roxanne and then get back on Vance's trail.

Fargo wasn't going to ignore the message, though, and he wasn't going to tell Vance what was going on. Their route from Fort Worth to San Antonio would take them south anyway. They would keep that rendezvous with the kidnappers, but Fargo didn't intend to let either Vance or Roxanne die.

He would need to have some surprises up his sleeve if they were all going to survive this day.

When he got back to the livery stable, he found that the supplies had been delivered from the general store, packed in several canvas bags.

"You'll need a packhorse, won't you, Mr. Fargo?" the liveryman asked. "I got a good one picked out for you."

Fargo agreed that the animal, a big hammer-headed roan, would be fine for carrying their supplies.

"We need another saddle horse, too," he said, bringing a puzzled frown to the stable owner's face.

"You mean to use as an extra mount?"

"That's right," Fargo said. Let the man think that. But if everything worked out, Roxanne would be riding that horse, not him or Vance Forrestal.

They settled on a chestnut gelding. Fargo had to buy tack for the horse, too. Like everything else, it went on Vance's account. The liveryman scratched his head a little worriedly.

"I *am* gonna get paid for all this, ain't I?"

"Vance is good for it," Fargo assured him, "and I reckon his pa would pay if he couldn't."

"Yeah, I guess. Although it wouldn't surprise me if one o' these days old Isaac was to, what do you call it, disinherit the boy."

"I don't think it'll ever come to that," Fargo said, although to be truthful, he had no real idea what the elder Forrestal might do if he became disgusted enough with his son.

Maybe if Fargo got Vance safely to San Antonio and the youngster wound up married to Sally Pryor, he would grow up some. Stranger things had been known to happen.

It wasn't Fargo's job to nurture Vance Forrestal's maturity, though. His task was keeping him alive long enough to marry the girl. What happened after that was up to Vance.

Once the horses were squared away, Fargo returned to the Gem to check out of his room and eat lunch before they hit the trail. He didn't have much of an appetite because he was worried about Roxanne, but he knew she would be safe enough for a while, as long as the kidnappers had a potential use for her.

The pretty blond waitress, Margaret, was still working in the hotel dining room. She smiled at Fargo and said, "If you're going to be around for a while, I get off work at three o'clock. I'd purely admire to take a walk along the bluff with you, Mr. Fargo."

"I'd enjoy that, too," Fargo said honestly, "but I'm afraid I'll be gone from Fort Worth by then."

She looked disappointed.

"If you ever ride through this way again, you be sure to look me up," she said.

"I'll do that," Fargo promised with a nod.

He ate fried chicken and potatoes but didn't really taste them. When he was finished, he walked out of the hotel with his saddlebags slung over his shoulder and his Henry rifle in his hand.

Margaret gave him a wistful little smile as he left.

Vance Forrestal was waiting at the livery stable when Fargo got there. He wore boots, denim trousers, a butternut shirt, and a broad-brimmed brown hat.

"How's this for a traveling outfit?" he asked.

"It'll do," Fargo replied with a nod. "You just need one more thing . . ."

He found the Colt he had bought among the supplies and handed the belt and holster to Vance.

"Strap that on. There's a rifle like mine there for you, too."

Vance buckled the belt around his hips and took

hold of the gun butt. He raised and lowered the weapon a couple of times without taking it out of the holster.

"It's heavy," he said.

"You'll get used to it," Fargo assured him. "We'll work with it along the way, once we get away from Fort Worth."

A smile lit up Vance's face at that prospect.

"You mean you'll teach me how to be a shootist?"

"Don't set your sights too high," Fargo drawled. "I'd settle for teaching you not to shoot your foot off when you draw."

"I can do better than that," Vance scoffed.

"We'll see."

Hostlers brought out the three saddle horses and the pack animal. Vance pointed at the extra mount and asked, "Why do we need three horses?"

"Better to have one you don't need than need one you don't have," Fargo said.

"Wisdom according to Skye Fargo, the Trailsman."

"Wisdom according to a lot of fellas who might have died but stayed alive instead," Fargo countered.

Vance shrugged, grasped the dun's reins, and swung up into the saddle.

They moved out with Fargo leading the pack-horse and the extra saddle mount. The bluff overlooking the river was on the north side of town. On the south, the landscape sloped much more gently down to a broad plain.

Fargo knew their route would follow a natural border of sorts, with flat land stretching out to the east and terrain that gradually grew more rugged and hilly to the west. East Texas was largely settled, with quite a few towns and an abundance of farms. From here on west, however, settlement was sparse and the threat of Indians was much greater. It wasn't far from here, in fact, where the massive plateau known for good reason as Comanche Peak was located.

They had gone a couple of miles from town when Vance said proudly, "See? I told you I could ride."

"Tell me that again in three hundred miles," Fargo said. "Got any whiskey?"

Vance grinned broadly.

"As a matter of fact, I do. You want a swig?"

Fargo held out his hand. Vance reached into his saddlebags and brought out a fancy silver flask. He handed it to Fargo.

The Trailsman used his teeth to pull the cork. Then, without any warning, he upended the flask and began pouring out the potent liquid inside it.

"Hey!" Vance yelped. "What the hell are you doing?"

"I don't plan on spending ten days on the trail with somebody who's drunk," Fargo said bluntly. "You hired me to get you safely to San Antonio, and this is the first step."

"You can't expect me to travel without liquor! You drink, you damned hypocrite! I saw you with my own eyes, in the Top Notch!"

"First of all, mind how you talk to me," Fargo said, his voice growing flinty. "Second, you were so drunk while you were in the Top Notch that you shouldn't trust anything you think you saw there. As it happens, though, I do take a drink when the notion strikes me. I can do without it, though, when I need to."

"I'm impressed as all hell," Vance practically snarled. "That still doesn't give you the right to pour out my whiskey."

"Maybe not." Fargo reined in and took the flask in his left hand. He tossed it high in the air above their heads.

His right hand flashed down to his hip and palmed out the Colt. Three shots blasted from it, and with each report, the flask jerked in the air as a bullet tore through it. When it thudded to the ground, there were three neat holes in it.

"Maybe you can learn to shoot like that someday, if you stay sober long enough," Fargo said.

Vance gaped at the ruined flask for a few seconds, then said, "Do you know how much that cost?"

"Take it out of my pay," Fargo said as he reloaded the spent chambers. He holstered the gun. "Let's go. And by the way, when we stop tonight, you'll pour out any more Who-hit-John you've got stashed away in our gear."

Vance muttered some curses, but he didn't argue. Not after that display of gun speed and marksmanship.

They pushed on, Fargo keeping an estimate in his head of how far they had come. The note the old-timer had passed along had said that the kidnappers would be waiting at a grove of big trees ten miles south of Fort Worth. Fargo hoped to spot those trees before they were close enough for the kidnappers to see him and Vance.

Late in the afternoon, as they topped one of the long rises in the rolling landscape, Fargo noticed a dark mass to one side of the trail about a mile ahead. He reined in sharply.

"Hold on a minute," he said to Vance.

"What's wrong?" the young man asked as he brought the dun to a halt.

"Something up there I want to take a look at."

Fargo dug in his saddlebags and found the pair of army field glasses that he carried. He lifted them to his eyes and peered through the lenses.

What he had seen was a clump of large oak trees to the right of the trail. The oaks were tall, with thick trunks, and they were the largest trees Fargo had seen since leaving Fort Worth. He figured that he and Vance had come about nine miles, too, which would put the oak grove in the right place.

He put away the glasses and backed the Ovaro away from the crest, motioning for Vance to follow him. When they were out of sight of the trees, Fargo said, "Here's what we're going to do. You're going to lead the packhorse and ride on by yourself for a spell. There's something I have to take care of."

"What?"

Fargo shook his head.

"You don't need to know that. Just follow the trail, and I'll join back up with you after a while."

Vance's face hardened with anger.

"You're deserting me," he accused. "You're giving up on the job."

"No, I'm not," Fargo said. "You've got my word, you'll see me in a little while. Just ride on the way we've been going."

A note of hysteria crept into Vance's voice as he said, "Something's wrong. This is a trap of some sort. Damn it, Fargo, if you've double-crossed me—"

Fargo bit back a curse as he saw that this wasn't going to work. He was going to have to take Vance into his confidence and tell him about Roxanne's abduction and the note from the kidnappers.

That meant, ultimately, that he was going to have to place his own safety, and that of Roxanne, in the hands of a young wastrel who had whiskey for blood and about as much gumption as a snail.

They would be lucky if any of them lived long enough to see the sun go down this evening.

5

"Listen," Fargo said emphatically. "We're riding into trouble, Vance, and I reckon you might as well know about it."

"I knew it!" the young man exclaimed. "What's happened, Skye?"

"You remember that girl Roxanne?"

Vance frowned.

"You mean the whore who works at the Top Notch? I've seen her around. I've never been upstairs with her, though, if that's what you mean."

"It's not," Fargo said. "I just wanted to make sure you know who I'm talking about. She's been kidnapped."

Vance's eyes widened in surprise.

"Who'd want to kidnap a whore? And what's that got to do with us?"

"I'm pretty sure the kidnappers are those other two men who are after you," Fargo explained. "The ones you say were hired by Big Nate Pryor to kill you. They may have recruited a few more men to help them, too."

Vance shook his head in confusion.

"I still don't understand. Why would they kidnap this Roxanne? *I'm* the one they're after."

"They know that you and I are traveling together. They must have spies around Fort Worth whose job it was to find out your plans. And they know that Roxanne and I were together last night."

A lecherous grin spread across Vance's face.

"You mean when you went with her in the Top Notch . . . or later?"

"Later, not that it's any of your business," Fargo snapped. "Well, as it turns out, maybe it *is* a little of your business, indirectly at least. Because those bastards grabbed Roxanne and sent a note to me implying that I had to turn you over to them or they'd kill her."

"But you're not going to do that." Vance's eyes grew wide again, with horror this time. "You're not, are you? Or is that it? Is this the double cross?"

"There's no double cross," Fargo said. "I want to work things so that both you and Roxanne make it through this, and me, too, for that matter. That's why we're splitting up."

"I don't understand."

Fargo made an effort to hold on to his patience. It wasn't easy.

"Up ahead about a mile, there's a grove of big oak trees on the right side of the trail. That's where they're waiting for us with Roxanne. They probably figure they'll work a trade, you for her, but once they've got their hands on you, they'll try to kill us all. That's how they hope it'll work out, anyway."

"But we're going to keep them from doing that," Vance guessed.

"I'm going to circle around to the west and come at them from behind," Fargo explained. "Give me a little time, and then you come riding along bold as brass."

"Won't they wonder where you are?"

"They'll wonder," Fargo agreed with a nod, "but

you're their main target, remember? If they kill you, they get their money. And that's all they really care about."

The color was leaving Vance's face.

"So you're saying they'll start shooting at me as soon as I ride up."

"Probably. But when they open up on you, I'll hit them from behind."

"Oh, I'm sure that'll do me a lot of good," Vance said sarcastically. "I'll be shot to ribbons by then."

"Not if you move fast enough. There's a gully on the other side of the trail, across from those trees. Get into it as quick as you can, and it'll give you some cover."

"What if they hit me with their first shot?"

Fargo smiled.

"We'll hope their aim's not that good."

Vance sighed and shook his head.

"This is crazy. We're risking our lives—my life more than yours, actually—for the sake of some prostitute? Was she really that good in bed, Skye?"

"She may not be innocent in the ways of the world," Fargo said, "but she's sure not to blame for any of the mess she finds herself in. I can't sit by and do nothing while those bastards kill her."

"What if I stay here and you circle around behind them like you said?" Vance suggested. "You can still take them by surprise and rescue the girl."

"The odds will be a lot higher that way. I need their attention focused on you." Fargo shrugged. "But if you won't do it, I can't force you. I can ride on when this is over, though, and you can make your way to San Antonio by yourself."

"Wait a minute," Vance said quickly. "Don't get carried away. Isn't it likely that if these men fail, Big Nate will just send more killers after me?"

"You know him a whole heap better than I do. What do you think?"

Vance took a deep breath and nodded.

"That's exactly what he would do. I won't be safe until Sally and I are married."

"It's a risk no matter what you do," Fargo pointed out. "But if we work together, we'll stand a better chance of making it through."

Vance thought it over for a long moment before finally nodding slowly.

"All right. I'll distract them by riding along the trail like I'm not expecting trouble. But instead of waiting for them to take a free shot at me, why don't we time it so that you can get into position and start shooting first? That'll distract them from *me,* and I'll have a better chance to reach that gully."

That wrinkle in the plan had already occurred to Fargo, and he was glad to see that Vance had thought of it, too. He smiled as he nodded.

"Those are good tactics. There may be hope for you yet, Vance."

"Please, don't give me so much praise," Vance said. "It's liable to go to my head."

Fargo ignored that acid comment and said, "When the shooting starts, just keep your head down and leave your gun in its holster."

"You don't want my help?"

"I don't want to have to worry about getting shot accidentally. Just stay low in that gully, and I'll come get you when it's all over."

"What if it's not you, but one of those killers?"

"Then I guess you'll have to use that Colt after all," Fargo said.

He left Vance there with instructions to wait fifteen minutes before riding down toward the grove of oak trees. Taking the extra horse with him, Fargo headed west.

The kidnappers no doubt would be puzzled by

his absence, but if they saw Vance riding along leading a packhorse, they might not suspect anything. They might even decide that Fargo had cut Vance loose and left him to make the trip to San Antonio by himself.

If that was the case, they were likely to be overconfident about their ambush. Fargo would take any edge he could get.

He pushed the Ovaro, wanting to get behind the kidnappers in plenty of time. When he judged that he was getting close, he stopped and tied the extra mount's reins to a sturdy bush. He would return when the shooting was over and retrieve the horse.

And if by some chance he wasn't able to do that, eventually the horse would be able to pull free and return to the stable in Fort Worth. But that would mean Fargo was dead, so he put that thought out of his mind.

He rode ahead, moving at a slower and quieter pace now. He topped a small knoll and saw the grove of oaks below him, about two hundred yards away. Sure enough, several saddled horses stood riderless at the rear edge of the trees, with one man holding their reins.

Fargo drew his Henry rifle from its saddle sheath and looked toward the trail. There was Vance, riding along at a leisurely pace, the packhorse following behind him.

The youngster had some acting ability, Fargo thought. He looked like he didn't have a care in the world. Anyone watching him wouldn't guess that he knew he was riding into an ambush.

Fargo could tell from the tense attitude of the man holding the horses that something was about to happen. He figured the trap was about to be sprung. In one smooth movement, the Trailsman brought the rifle to his shoulder and fired.

The bullet screamed over the head of the horse-holder and made the man jump crazily. When he landed, he jerked his gun from its holster and started blazing away at the knoll where Fargo sat on the Ovaro, even though the range was too great for a handgun.

Fargo had put the first shot over the man's head just in case he was reading the situation wrong and the man didn't have anything to do with the ambush. That violent reaction banished any doubt from Fargo's mind. He dropped his aim when he fired again. This time the lead slammed through the man's shoulder and knocked him to the ground, putting him out of the fight.

Fargo jammed his boot heels into the Ovaro's sides and sent the big stallion plunging down the slope in a headlong gallop.

From the corner of his eye Fargo saw Vance Forrestal racing his horse toward the gully on the far side of the trail. Guns began to blast from the grove of trees, but Vance was a fast-moving target now and much harder to hit.

Fargo held his fire as he rode toward the oaks. He didn't know where Roxanne was, and if he fired blindly into the trees, he might hit her. Instead, he hoped that the earlier shots from their rear would draw the kidnappers into the open, and as he approached, that was just what happened. Two men ran out of the trees, shooting toward him with rifles.

The hurricane deck of a racing horse was no place to take accurate aim, even when the horse had as smooth a gait as the Ovaro. Fargo held his fire and leaned forward over the stallion's neck, making himself as small a target as possible. Bullets whined overhead and kicked up dust around the Ovaro's thudding hooves, but none of the slugs found their mark.

When Fargo thought he was close enough, he

left the saddle in a rolling dive and came up on one knee, the Henry spitting flame and lead as he fired from the hip. The rifle's lever was a blur as Fargo worked it between each round.

The bullets tore through the bodies of the two gunmen and drove them backward. They collapsed in bloody heaps. Almost before they hit the ground, Fargo was up and running toward the trees.

He ducked into the grove and drew the Colt. The heavy revolver was more suited for this sort of close work. So far he hadn't caught a glimpse of Roxanne. He felt sure she was somewhere in the trees—and so were more gunmen.

The ground under the oaks was littered with small, broken branches and old, dried leaves from the previous autumn. It was impossible to move without making some sound, but Fargo came as close to it as humanly possible. He cat-footed through the trees, ready for trouble.

It came quickly enough, with a rush from his left. He spun as a gun blared and a bullet knocked a chunk of bark from the tree trunk behind his head. He saw a man in a black-and-white cowhide vest throwing down on him and triggered a shot before the man could fire again.

The gunman grunted and doubled over like a hairpin, bending at the waist. He collapsed, shot through the belly.

The two men Fargo suspected of having masterminded Roxanne's kidnapping had indeed hired more help, just as Fargo had speculated they might. So far he had shot four men, and there had to be at least one more in the trees, because he still hadn't seen Roxanne.

"Fargo! Damn you, Fargo, show yourself or—"

The man who issued the threat in a harsh voice didn't go on. Instead a scream of pain rang out.

Roxanne.

Fargo's jaw tightened. He had set up this attack from behind in hopes of freeing Roxanne. All his efforts would go for naught if he stood by and allowed her to be hurt or killed.

"Take it easy," he said, his voice taut with anger but carrying easily through the trees. "No need to hurt the girl. This is between you and me, mister."

The kidnapper was ahead of him somewhere. The man said, "I won't just hurt the girl. I'll kill her unless you keep coming forward into a clearing up ahead of you. And come with your hands empty, or I swear I'll put a bullet through this whore's head!"

Roxanne surprised Fargo by shouting, "Don't listen to him, Skye! Kill the son of a—"

A thud cut short her defiant words, and knowing that the gunman had just struck her sent a surge of fresh anger flooding through Fargo's veins.

That bastard had plenty to answer for. Right now, though, Fargo had to do what he could to save Roxanne's life.

He leaned the Henry against a tree and holstered the Colt. Having his hands empty at a moment like this was a bad feeling, but there was nothing he could do about it. He started forward, no longer being careful not to make any noise. The twigs and leaves crunched loudly under his boots.

As he came to a small clearing within the grove of oak trees, he spotted Roxanne on the other side of the open space. A man stood behind her with his left arm held tightly and cruelly around her throat. His right hand pressed a gun to her head. She looked scared to death and had a bruise forming on her cheek, but she seemed to be unharmed otherwise.

Fargo couldn't see much of the man using Roxanne as a shield—his arms, part of a shoulder, half of a whiskery, merciless face. He wore a black hat with a tall, rounded crown.

"Stop right there, Fargo!" the kidnapper ordered as Fargo stepped into the clearing. "You're a damn fool, you know it? You never should've thrown in with that worthless young Forrestal boy."

"Because Nate Pryor hired you to kill him?" Fargo asked coldly.

"I ain't sayin' nothin' about that. All I'm sayin' is you're about to get yourself killed for a fella who ain't anywhere near worth it."

Fargo expected the kidnapper to pull the gun away from Roxanne's head at any second and blaze away at him. His hope was that he could throw himself aside and draw his Colt while Roxanne took advantage of the opportunity to twist out of the man's grip. If she did that, Fargo would have a shot . . .

"Hey!"

The unexpected shout came from behind the gunman. Fargo's eyes jerked in that direction, and he saw Vance Forrestal advancing through the trees, six-gun leveled in his outthrust hand.

Clearly, Vance had a hard time following orders.

"Let her go or I'll kill you!" Vance threatened.

Instinct made the gunman swing toward him. As he did so, the gun came away from Roxanne's head for a second.

That was long enough for her to act. She managed to lower her head and sink her teeth in the arm around her neck.

The gunman howled in pain as Roxanne bit him savagely. He slashed at her head with the gun. Before the blow could fall, Fargo was there, having launched himself across the clearing.

Fargo crashed into the two of them, knocking Roxanne out of the man's grip. As they all sprawled to the ground, Fargo hoped that Vance had sense enough to hold his fire. If the young man started pulling the trigger, he was liable to shoot all of them.

Fargo twisted on the ground and hammered a punch into the gunman's face. The man responded by kicking him in the belly. For a second, Fargo was numb and couldn't breathe. The gunman scrambled up and tried to run, but Fargo's muscles began to work again and he was able to lunge forward and trip the man up.

The gunman rolled over and came up with a broken branch in his hand. He swung it at Fargo's head, forcing the Trailsman to duck and let the blow go over his head. Fargo dove forward, tackling the man around the waist.

For long moments they wrestled desperately. Fargo was bigger and probably stronger, but the gunman was quick and wiry and hard to hang on to. He got a hand on Fargo's face and tried to gouge his eyes out. Fargo heaved up from the ground and tossed him to one side.

The gunman was a shade faster getting to his knees. In his hands he clutched a flat, sharp rock about the diameter of a dinner plate. He loomed over Fargo, ready to smash the rock down with deadly force on Fargo's skull.

A gun roared before the man could strike. Fargo saw the spurt of blood from the front of the man's shirt as a bullet tore all the way through him from the back. The rock slipped from the man's fingers and thudded to the ground. Crimson trickled from the corner of his mouth.

Then he pitched forward onto his face, and the limp, lifeless way that he fell told Fargo he was dead.

Vance still stood off to the side, mouth open, gun hanging from his hand. Nearby, Roxanne stood with a gun in her hand, too, but smoke curled from the barrel of the weapon she held. She had fired the fatal shot.

Fargo knew the gunman must have dropped his Colt while they were struggling. Roxanne had scooped it up and waited for an opportunity. She had fired to save Fargo's life.

He sat up, then pushed himself to his feet. Glancing at Vance, he said, "Put your gun away."

Vance looked at the Colt in his hand like he had forgotten that he was holding it.

"Oh," he said. He slid the revolver back in the holster on his hip.

"Skye, are you all right?" Roxanne asked.

"I'm fine. What about you?"

She nodded as she lowered the gun in her hand.

"That bastard hit me and roughed me up some, but I'm not really hurt. I was just scared."

"With good reason," Fargo told her. "They would have killed us all, if they'd gotten the chance." He drew his Colt. "You two stay here while I check on the others."

Maybe Vance would actually stay put this time, he thought as he moved into the trees.

The man in the cowhide vest was dead, as was another of the men Fargo had downed in his initial attack. The other two were gone, though, and so were some of the horses.

He knew he had only wounded the man holding the horses. The man must have been able to grab one of the mounts and ride off despite having a bullet-shattered shoulder. Obviously, the other missing man had only been wounded, too, and had caught one of the other horses.

Fargo didn't like the fact that two of the enemy had gotten away, but at least they had suffered some fairly serious wounds and probably didn't represent a threat anymore. He went back to the clearing and said to Vance, "Why didn't you stay in that gully like I told you?"

"I thought I might be able to help," Vance replied with a shrug. "It sounded like a war going on in here."

"A small war, I reckon. Next time, do as you're told."

"I will," Vance promised with a nod.

Fargo didn't quite believe him, though. Vance Forrestal was accustomed to doing whatever he wanted to, following whatever whim occurred to him.

"I couldn't let you get killed," Vance added. "You haven't taught me how to shoot yet."

Roxanne looked at him in surprise.

"You jump into the middle of a gunfight and you don't even know how to shoot?"

"Well, I *have* shot a gun before. Not one like this, mind you, but I do know which end the bullets come out of, after all."

Fargo could have told her that she'd be wasting her time trying to have a sensible talk with Vance, but he didn't bother. Instead he said, "Let's round up our horses."

The Ovaro came to his whistle, of course, and once he was mounted it didn't take Fargo long to fetch the extra saddle mount he and Vance had brought with them.

"What do we do with these bodies?" Vance asked as they mounted up.

"There are plenty of coyotes and buzzards around," Fargo said. "They'll take care of them."

Vance looked shocked.

"You're not going to report this to the law?"

"No point in it," Fargo said. "They were trying to kill us, so we acted in self-defense. We don't need an inquest to tell us that. Besides, we'd lose at least a day doing that, and we've got a far piece to go."

"I suppose you're right. It just seems . . . uncivilized somehow."

"Sometimes civilization is overrated." Fargo turned to Roxanne. He noticed that she had stripped the gun belt off the man she had killed and buckled it around her hips. It was a little big, but not so much that she couldn't make do. She wore a sleeping gown that was thin enough her dark brown nipples showed through it. "Fort Worth is only ten miles or so back up the trail. You should be able to make it without any trouble."

Roxanne shook her head.

"The hell with that. I'm going with you two."

The bold declaration took Fargo by surprise. He gave a little shake of his head and said, "How do you figure that?"

"I don't have any family or anything else holding me to Fort Worth. I've been ready to shake off the dust of that place for a while. Besides, I'm scared to go back."

"Why? Bullock's not going to do anything—"

"I'm not afraid of Bullock. I'm afraid of whoever it is that wants the two of you dead. I've already been kidnapped once by somebody who wanted to use me as a weapon against you, Skye."

Fargo said, "That's not going to happen again."

"How can you be certain of that?"

"If you're trying to avoid danger, then Skye and I aren't the best companions for you," Vance pointed out. "More than likely there'll be more trouble along the way."

"And I'd rather face it with you boys around," Roxanne insisted.

Fargo frowned as he thought about what she was saying. He doubted if any of his and Vance's enemies would bother her again if she returned to Fort Worth . . . but he couldn't guarantee that. It was possible, though unlikely, that some more of Big Nate Pryor's hired guns would grab her again to use against Fargo. That ploy had almost worked once.

And Roxanne was strong willed; he knew that about her. The fact that she had killed a man a few minutes earlier didn't seem to bother her all that much. If Fargo refused to take her along, she might follow on her own. That definitely *would* be more dangerous for her.

"You can ride with us for a ways," he said, coming to a decision. "Maybe as far as Waco."

Vance stared at him.

"Are you sure that's a good idea, Skye?"

"No, I pretty well figure it's a bad idea," Fargo replied with a faint smile. "But if you're about to get married, you ought to know by now that arguing with a woman is a pure-dee waste of time."

Roxanne smiled smugly.

"I might take offense at that comment," she said, "if it wasn't true."

"Come on," Fargo said. He led the way out onto the trail again and headed south. They were leading the horses belonging to the three dead kidnappers. Spare mounts would come in handy on a long ride like this, and under the circumstances, Fargo figured they had as much right to the animals as anybody.

He looked over at Roxanne. She was riding astraddle, with her gown pulled up over her calves. Her breasts bobbed slightly under the thin fabric.

"This isn't going to work," Fargo said. "The first settlement we come to, you'll positively scandalize the place, dressed like that."

"Undressed like that is more like it," Vance put in.

Roxanne shrugged, which made her breasts move even more.

"This is what I was wearing when those bastards climbed into my room and took me out of there."

That reminded Fargo of something.

"I found some bloodstains on the floor of your room. Not your blood, I reckon?"

"No, I managed to get hold of a knife and cut one of them. I wish I could have carved his heart out. But another one grabbed me and knocked the knife out of my hand, and they pulled a sack over my head so I could barely breathe. After a while I couldn't fight them anymore."

"Did they . . ." Vance began tentatively.

"Line up to give me a poke once they had me away from town?" Roxanne said when he didn't finish the question. "No, they didn't get around to it. They were too busy trying to figure out how they were going to kill you. Don't go thinking I'm some sort of blushing virgin just because that bunch didn't have their way with me, though."

Vance held up a hand.

"The thought never entered my mind, I swear."

Fargo shook his head, figuring the long ride to San Antonio had just gotten longer. He reined in. "Let's go through our gear. I reckon we've got a spare shirt and a pair of pants that'll fit you good enough, Roxanne. Next settlement we come to we'll buy you a pair of boots."

She smiled at him.

"Are you sure you want to cover me up like that, Skye?"

Fargo looked at the lines of her body visible through the gown and thought about what a distraction she was going to be. A pleasant distraction, to be sure, but still a distraction.

"I'm damned sure."

6

Even wearing a man's shirt with the sleeves rolled
up and trousers that were too baggy for her, Roxanne looked mighty fetching, Fargo thought. The
gun belt strapped around her hips didn't really distract from that appeal, either.

By evening they came to a settlement called Buchanan, according to the wood-burned sign nailed
to a tree. The community had several churches, a
school, a squat stone building that functioned as
the Johnson County Courthouse, and a main street
lined with businesses that stretched for two blocks.

Fargo hoped they could find some boots or shoes
to fit Roxanne. The three travelers reined to a halt
in front of a general store that was still open. Fargo
looked around in the dusk and saw a saloon across
the street.

"You two go inside and find Roxanne something
to wear on her feet," he said.

"Where are you going?" Vance asked.

Fargo nodded toward the saloon.

"Thought I'd mosey over there for a spell."

"I knew it!" Vance exclaimed. "Mister High-
and-Mighty, No-Whiskey-Allowed, and the first
place you head as soon as we get to a town is the
nearest saloon!"

"Settle down," Fargo said, his voice an irritated

growl. "I want to find out if those two wounded men showed up here, and a saloon's usually the best place to get information."

"Oh," Vance said, somewhat mollified. "I guess that makes sense."

Fargo looked at Roxanne.

"Can I trust you to keep an eye on him?"

"Sure, I won't let him out of my sight," she promised.

As he dismounted, Vance muttered something about turning over the responsibility for him to a whore, but both Fargo and Roxanne ignored him. Fargo looped the Ovaro's reins around the hitch rail, then started across the street toward the saloon.

The place was called the Double Eagle. Fargo had been in hundreds of saloons just like it. He walked over to the hardwood bar and nodded to the apron, a burly man with sparse red hair.

"Beer," Fargo said.

The bartender drew the beer, and set it in front of Fargo. "Just passin' through?"

Fargo nodded and sampled the beer, then nodded again to indicate that it was good.

"On my way south," he said. "Heading for San Antonio."

"Heard it's a nice place. Never been there, myself."

Fargo nursed the beer along for a few more minutes of idle talk as he looked around the saloon. There were only about a dozen patrons, a mixture of townsmen and farmers. He didn't see any women.

"I noticed a couple of fellas on the road earlier this afternoon," he commented after a while. "They looked like they had run into some trouble and maybe were hurt. They were headed in this direction in a hurry. I was just wondering what happened to them."

"I haven't seen anybody like that," the bartender said, "but unless they rode right past my front window, I wouldn't have seen 'em. Doc Pierce would know. He's our only medico here in town."

"Where's his office?"

"Next block, other side of the street, over the hardware store."

Fargo nodded his thanks for the information, then gave a casual shrug.

"I'm not sure I'm curious enough to go to that much trouble," he said. "None of my business, after all."

The bartender seemed to accept that. He pointed at Fargo's empty mug and asked, "Another one?"

"No, this'll do me for now. Much obliged."

He left a coin on the bar to pay for the beer and strolled to the batwinged entrance. As he emerged from the Double Eagle, he saw Vance Forrestal and Roxanne coming out of the store across the street.

Roxanne wore boots now, and a broad-brimmed black hat with silver decorations around the band. Fargo smiled. She didn't look much like a prostitute anymore, although the proud thrust of her breasts under the man's shirt made it obvious she was a woman.

Fargo joined them. "I'm still trying to scout up some information about those two missing hardcases. You can go get something to eat if you want."

"You know I don't have any money," Roxanne said. "Vance paid for these boots and this hat."

"And he can buy your supper, too," Fargo said. "Isn't that right, Vance?"

"Of course," Vance agreed without hesitation.

"I'm responsible for all the expenses on this trip . . . although I didn't think a, ah, lady of the evening would be one of them."

Roxanne snapped, "You ain't hirin' me for that. I'm just along for the ride. And I don't mean it *that way,* either."

Vance held up his hands in surrender.

"I'm sorry. I didn't mean any offense."

"Just watch what you say around me," Roxanne warned him. "I may not be a lady, but I'm still a gal."

And a mighty nice-looking one, Fargo thought, but he didn't say anything. He still had work to do.

He left Vance and Roxanne at a hash house and climbed the outside stairs attached to the building where the hardware store was located. A light burned in the second-floor office of the local doctor.

A sign on the door at the top of the stairs said to go on in, so Fargo did. He found a middle-aged man with wispy fair hair sitting at a desk, reading a medical book. The man lowered the book and looked up at Fargo.

"You appear to be a healthy enough specimen," the doctor said. "What can I do for you, son?"

"I'm not sick or hurt, Doc. I was just wondering if you'd had a couple of gunshot patients this afternoon."

"And what business of yours would that be?" the doctor asked, raising his eyebrows. Before Fargo could answer, he continued, "No, wait, let me guess. You're the one who put them in that condition."

Fargo could see that this physician was sharp-witted enough so that there wasn't any point in trying to put anything over on him. He nodded. "That's right. They ambushed me and some friends of mine back up the trail toward Fort Worth. We swapped lead with them and came out ahead on the deal."

That was close enough to the truth, he thought. No need to mention the kidnapping angle.

"Well, if you're worried that they might be lying in wait for you here in town, I suppose you can rest easy. I haven't seen them. I'm friends with the local law, too, and the sheriff would have mentioned it to me if he'd seen any shot-up strangers in Buchanan."

Fargo nodded, satisfied with the answer.

"Thanks, Doc. I won't sleep with both eyes open tonight."

"One will do, eh?"

Fargo grinned. The doctor had recognized him as the sort of man who didn't take any chances he didn't have to.

"Is there anything you need to report to the authorities?" the doctor went on.

"Not a thing," Fargo answered with a shake of his head.

"Well, then, I'll get back to my reading. A doctor never quits studying and learning."

Neither did a frontiersman, Fargo thought, leastways if he wanted to stay alive very long.

He walked back down to the hash house and joined Vance and Roxanne. They were halfway through their supper, but Fargo was hungry enough so that he caught up fairly quickly.

"Are we staying here in town tonight?" Vance asked.

"I reckon that'll be all right," Fargo said after thinking for a moment. "I saw a decent-looking hotel down the street. Might as well take advantage of it now while we can, since we'll probably be spending a lot of other nights on the trail."

"That's what I thought." Vance inclined his head toward Roxanne. "And we've the, ah, lady to think of . . ."

"I told you I'm not a lady," she snapped. "And I've slept on the ground, with nothing but the stars over my head, more than once in my life."

"You'll get the chance to again," Fargo assured her. "For tonight, I say we get the best hotel room Vance's money can buy."

"Agreed," Vance said.

They finished their meals and walked down the street to the Brackett Hotel. Fargo would have gotten a room for Roxanne and one for him and Vance, but before he could speak up Vance asked for three rooms. If he wanted to spring for that, Fargo wasn't going to stop him.

The clerk gave them three rooms on the second floor, two of them next to each other and the third room across the hall. Fargo told Vance and Roxanne to go on up while he took care of getting all their horses stabled.

When he finished that chore and went up to the second floor of the hotel, Vance called to him through the open door of the single room to the left of the corridor.

"That's your room there, next to the lady's," Vance said, pointing.

"All right," Fargo said with a nod. "I left it to you and Roxanne to figure out who was staying where."

Vance leered.

"I wouldn't count on her staying in her own room all night, if you know what I mean. She seems quite fond of you, Skye, and after all, you've already been with her . . ."

"That's up to her," Fargo said.

"If it would help, I could slip her a little extra money."

Fargo gave him a hard look and said, "You know, sometimes I wonder if a good swift kick in the ass might knock some sense into that brain of yours."

"My brain's in my head, not in my—Oh, now I understand." Vance held up his hands. "But I'm not insulted. I suppose I deserved that. There are some things the lady doesn't need to be reminded of."

"And you could stop using that word *lady* so smug-like, too," Fargo pointed out. "Her name is Roxanne."

"All right, Skye. I'm sorry."

Fargo regarded the young man narrowly.

"Just don't make me sorry I agreed to help you," he said. "Now shut your door and get some sleep. We'll be back on the trail by sunup tomorrow."

With that Fargo went into his room and closed the door. Vance Forrestal was an arrogant young bastard. Fargo hadn't decided yet if there was anything worthwhile in him or not.

But by the time they got to San Antonio, if they made it that far, he ought to know, one way or the other.

Fargo stripped off his clothes, washed up from a basin that was on the small table in the hotel room, and stretched out on the bed. It was a warm night, so he lay on top of the covers, rather than under them. A faint breeze came in through the window.

The Colt was under his pillow tonight, even closer to hand than usual. As he lay there letting drowsiness steal over him, Fargo thought about the two gunmen who had gotten away.

Both men were wounded fairly seriously; he was sure of that. It was possible they had ridden off only to topple from their horses and die not long after they were out of sight.

But it was also feasible that they had survived and gotten help somewhere else. There were quite a few farms in the area, and Texans prided themselves on their hospitality. A couple of wounded men would be taken care of, if at all possible.

In that case, Fargo was confident that they would get word to Big Nate Pryor that their mission to stop Vance Forrestal had failed. And as soon as that knowledge reached Pryor, he would send out more men to waylay them. It was likely that danger would dog their trail all the way to San Antonio, Fargo thought.

He was half asleep when the soft knock sounded on his door. Instantly, he was awake, and his hand slipped under the pillow to close around the butt of the Colt. He swung his legs out of bed and stood up. Silently, he went to the door.

He said nothing. Calling out in answer to a knock like that might be a good way of getting a load of buckshot blasted right through the door. He listened intently, and after a moment he heard Roxanne call quietly, "Skye? Skye, are you awake?"

He couldn't detect any strain in her voice, so he didn't think anybody had a gun to her head, forcing her to knock on his door. Still, he was cautious. He turned the knob and stepped quickly to the side as he opened the door.

"Don't worry," she said with amusement in her voice. "I'm alone."

"Can't be too careful," Fargo said.

"You can see I'm not hiding anything," Roxanne said as she stood there in the doorway, silhouetted by the light from the lamp at the end of the corridor.

That light poured through the thin gown she wore and revealed the clean, smooth lines of her body. She stepped into the room after a moment, and Fargo swung the door shut behind them. Now the only light came through the window from the street outside.

"You expected me, didn't you?" Roxanne went on.

"I thought you might pay me a visit," Fargo said. "I was leaving it up to you, though."

She moved closer, a pale shape in the dim light.

"I couldn't stay away. Not after last night, and not after the way you risked your life to rescue me today."

"You wouldn't have been in danger if it hadn't been for Vance and me," Fargo pointed out.

"Maybe not, but you could have abandoned me. You didn't do that."

She was close enough now that he could feel the heat of her body. Her breath touched his bearded cheek. She reached up and put her arms around his neck, and her mouth found his in a sultry, searching kiss.

Fargo slipped his left arm around her waist and pulled her closer to him, pressing her body to his. He was nude and erect already, and she wore only the thin gown. It might as well not have been there as she ground her pelvis against his hard manhood.

Fargo broke the kiss and whispered, "You might ought to let me put this gun down before it accidentally goes off."

"I don't think Skye Fargo would ever let anything go off accidentally," she murmured. She lowered her head to his broad chest and began to kiss it. Her tongue circled one of his nipples before her lips closed around it and she began to suck.

Fargo steered her toward the bed. He put the gun on the table and then lowered Roxanne to the mattress. She pulled the gown up around her waist and spread her legs, opening herself for him in blatant invitation. Her profession had probably made her accustomed to that no-nonsense approach.

Tonight was different, though. Tonight she wasn't a soiled dove and he wasn't a customer. He wanted to make this last a while and mean something to her.

She made a little noise of surprise when he knelt between her wide-flung thighs and lowered his head to her femininity.

"Skye, what are you—"

Before she could finish the question, he had used his thumbs to open the fleshy folds, and there was no mistaking his intentions as he began to run his tongue up and down the moist opening.

Roxanne gasped and immediately grew even hotter and wetter. Skillfully, Fargo used his lips and tongue on her, even nipped lightly with his teeth at the little bud of flesh at the top of her opening. Roxanne cried out softly and her hips bucked up off the bed as Fargo did that.

He nuzzled through the thicket of dark hair as he continued lifting her higher and higher with his oral caresses. Her head thrashed from side to side on the pillow, and her fine breasts rose and fell rapidly as her breathing increased.

Her thighs pressed hard against the sides of his head as his tongue speared into her. Her hips pumped up and down as she climaxed. Fargo held on tight. The way her legs were wrapped around his head, there was no place he could go anyway.

Finally she slumped back and her thighs fell to the sides again. She was limp and out of breath as Fargo positioned himself over her. His shaft was as hard as a bar of iron. He placed the head against her drenched opening and entered her with a quick thrust of his hips, driving in all the way and filling her to the utmost.

Roxanne would have screamed if Fargo had not brought his mouth down on hers in a hard, passionate kiss at the very moment he penetrated her. He pressed his tongue into her mouth as his hips launched into a steady, pistonlike rhythm.

Locking her ankles together above his buttocks, Roxanne met Fargo thrust for thrust. Her breasts bobbed against his chest every time he surged into her. His shaft delved deeply into the opening between her legs, reaching her very core before withdrawing, only to penetrate again to her center.

Fargo's arousal quickly reached a point where he knew he couldn't continue for much longer. Clearly, Roxanne didn't want him to delay. She panted against his ear, "Give it to me, Skye! Oh, Lord! Give it to me!"

Fargo obliged, giving the mattress quite a workout as he bounced Roxanne's hips up and down on it. Her arms and legs twined tightly around him, and when she began to spasm around him, he surrendered to the climax that washed through him. Again and again his organ throbbed, showering her hotly with his seed.

As his culmination faded, so did hers, and she gave a long sigh of contentment. Fargo's weight sagged on her, flattening her breasts against his chest. She didn't seem to mind. In fact, when he tried to withdraw, she clutched him even tighter, keeping his softening manhood inside her.

Eventually they had to part, and when they did, Fargo rolled off and lay beside her. Both of them were breathless. Fargo reached over and cupped the breast closest to him, running his thumb over the hard brown nipple.

Roxanne returned the favor, cupping his now soft member in her hand. They lay there like that for long moments, gently caressing each other in the afterglow of the passion they had shared.

"My goodness, Skye," she whispered. "If every

gal had a man like you . . . well, the world would be a lot happier place, I reckon. Wouldn't be near as many wars."

Fargo chuckled.

"How do you figure that?"

She squeezed him tenderly.

"Because no woman would ever take a chance on her man getting killed. They'd put a stop to any fussing and fighting that was going on, right quick-like."

"Utopia," Fargo murmured.

"What's that?"

"Just a place," Fargo said. "Nice to think about, but I don't figure we'll ever get there."

"As long as you're there, that's the place I want to be," she whispered as she pillowed her head against his shoulder.

They went to sleep that way and dozed for a while.

Until they woke up and did it again . . . and again.

Fargo was tired the next morning, of course, but he had learned over the years that a fella bounced back pretty quickly from that sort of weariness. There was nothing like spending the night bedding a beautiful, eager woman to put some spring in a man's step.

Roxanne had slipped back over to her room long after midnight, so that both of them could get at least a few hours of uninterrupted sleep. She greeted him with a smile when she opened the door to his knock early the next morning. She was wearing that man's shirt and trousers again and was buckling on the gun belt.

Fargo had used the point of his Arkansas Toothpick to put another hole in the belt, so it fit her better now. She snugged it into place and said,

"Never thought I'd pack a pistol like this. I sort of like it, though."

"I don't reckon you're cut out to be a gunman," Fargo told her with a smile. "For one thing, you're not a man."

"And I'm bettin' that you're damned glad of that this morning, aren't you?"

"Can't argue with that," Fargo said. He stepped over to Vance's room and tapped on the door.

There was no answer.

Fargo frowned and rattled the knob.

"Vance?" he called.

Still no reply from inside. Fargo's features grew taut with worry.

"Is the door locked?" Roxanne sounded concerned, too, as she asked the question.

Fargo tried the knob. It turned easily, and he thrust the door open.

The sun wasn't up yet, but the sky outside had grown gray with the approach of dawn. There was enough light in the room for Fargo to tell that it was empty. Vance Forrestal was nowhere to be seen.

"Son of a bitch!" Fargo exploded.

He didn't know what could have happened to the young man. Vance had been armed, even though he didn't know how to use the pistol very well. If someone had broken into his room, all he would have had to do was to grab the gun and pull the trigger. The shots would have brought Fargo from across the hall. Even a loud yell would have done that.

Of course, Fargo reminded himself, he had been distracted by Roxanne part of the night. He glanced at her, suddenly suspicious, but then he discarded that idea just as quickly. Her own life had been in danger from the kidnappers the day before; she wouldn't be working with them now.

"What happened to him?" she asked, sounding every bit as puzzled as Fargo felt.

"I don't know. Bed's been slept in, you can tell that." Fargo's gaze darted around the room, swiftly taking in everything there was to be seen. "No signs of a fight. Furniture's not turned over, no blood on the floor."

"So he left on his own?"

"Maybe."

It was possible that Vance had woken up and gone downstairs in search of something to eat. Not that smart, but certainly possible.

"Come on," Fargo said, heading for the stairs.

There was no dining room in the hotel. Fargo asked the sleepy desk clerk, "Did the young fella who was with us already come downstairs this morning?"

"You mean Mr. Forrestal?" The clerk yawned and nodded. "He came down about thirty minutes ago and asked me about someplace to eat. There's a good café in the next block that opens early, so I sent him down there."

Fargo felt a moment of relief that was still touched with apprehension. Vance might be down at the café enjoying breakfast, but the possibility still existed that something had happened to him.

"Much obliged," he said as he started for the front door of the hotel. Roxanne followed.

"You think he's all right?" she asked when they came out on the boardwalk.

"No telling, but we ought to know soon," Fargo replied. His muscular legs carried him quickly toward the café. Roxanne hurried to keep up.

The sun was not yet up, but people were beginning to stir in Buchanan. A few horses plodded along the street, and an empty wagon rattled to a stop in front of the general store, driven by a farmer who had come into town for supplies.

Up ahead, the door of the café opened, and Vance Forrestal stepped out, apparently unharmed, working with a sliver of wood to get something out of his teeth.

Fargo took a deep breath, glad to see that Vance was all right. He intended to give the boy a good talking-to, though, and impress on him just how unwise it was to wander off alone like that.

But talk would have to wait, Fargo realized as his muscles suddenly stiffened. A figure had just stepped out of the shadowy mouth of an alley a few yards beyond Vance, and even in the gray light of dawn, the nickel-plated revolver in the man's hand glittered dangerously.

"Vance!" Fargo shouted as he reached for his Colt. "Get down!"

Fargo's draw was blindingly fast. Unfortunately, Vance's reaction to the shouted order wasn't. He stood there gaping at Fargo as the man in the alley mouth brought his gun up and fired.

A split second earlier, however, Fargo's revolver roared. With the angles what they were, he didn't have much room for the shot, and he had to count on Vance continuing to stand rooted there.

The bullet from Fargo's gun slashed through the air no more than six inches in front of Vance's face. It struck the would-be assassin just as the man pulled the trigger, clipping him on the left shoulder. The impact threw off his aim enough so that his slug hit the doorjamb next to Vance, chewing splinters off and into his cheeks.

Vance yelped and threw himself backward through the open door. With his intended target gone, the wounded gunman fired at Fargo instead, triggering a second shot that whipped past the Trailsman.

Coolly, Fargo fired a bullet into the bushwhacker's chest.

The man was thrown backward by the impact of the slug, arms and legs flung out to the side as he landed heavily on his back. He spasmed a couple of times, his limbs jerking grotesquely as death claimed him.

Fargo spun around, knowing that Roxanne had been behind him when the bushwhacker's second shot missed him. A curse welled up his throat at what he saw.

Roxanne was down, lying on the boardwalk with blood slowly darkening her shirt.

7

Fargo rammed the Colt back in its holster and sprang to Roxanne's side. He dropped to a knee and leaned over her.

She was unconscious. The bloodstain was on her left side, about halfway between her shoulder and her hip. Fargo pulled the Arkansas Toothpick from its sheath and used the keen blade to cut away the fabric of Roxanne's shirt, laying bare the wound.

A breath of relief hissed between Fargo's clenched teeth as he saw that the slug had just plowed a shallow furrow in Roxanne's side, rather than penetrating to her vitals. The wound was bloody and messy, but with any kind of luck, it wouldn't be life threatening.

A swift rataplan of footsteps sounded behind him and Fargo twisted around. His hand closed over the butt of the Colt, ready to draw it and meet any new danger.

But it was only Vance Forrestal, a shocked, worried expression on his face. Blood trickled from a cut on the young man's cheek.

"Skye!" he exclaimed. "Is Roxanne all right?"

"You can see she's not," Fargo replied curtly. "But it's not as bad as it looks." He nodded toward the cut on Vance's cheek. "What happened to you?"

Vance touched the blood on his face and looked at the red smear on his fingertips as if he hadn't been aware that he was hurt.

"One of those splinters from the post cut me, I guess," he said. "I don't know what else could have happened, and I remember my face stinging when that happened."

"Roxanne needs a doctor. Stay here with her while I fetch him."

Vance's look of worry intensified.

"But . . . but what if somebody else tries to kill me?"

"There's a gun on your hip," Fargo said grimly.

Vance swallowed hard but made no reply.

Fargo legged it down the street toward Dr. Pierce's office. His route took him past the dead bushwhacker. He paused and looked down at the man, studying the hard-bitten face.

He was convinced the man was one of the survivors from the group that had kidnapped Roxanne in Fort Worth. A bloodstained, makeshift bandage was wrapped around his midsection, Fargo saw as he bent over and pulled the man's shirt aside. That confirmed it as far as Fargo was concerned. The man had lived through the gunfight the day before . . .

But not this gunfight.

Dr. Pierce must have heard the shots, because he was already coming down the stairs when Fargo reached his office. The doctor carried his medical bag in one hand while he used the other to tuck his shirttails into his trousers.

"What happened?"

"A woman's been shot," Fargo told him. "Got a pretty deep graze on her side."

"Anybody else hurt?"

"One man—but you won't be able to help him."

Pierce grunted as he hurried down the street with Fargo at his side.

"Like that, is it? And I suppose you were responsible for the man's unfortunate condition, as you were with those fellows yesterday?"

"This hombre is one of the men I was asking you about," Fargo explained. "I guess he wanted to settle the score."

He left it at that, not offering any more details.

A small group of townspeople had gathered around Vance and Roxanne while Fargo was gone, drawn by the shots that had shattered the early morning peace. They stepped aside to let the doctor get to Roxanne.

He knelt beside her and examined the wound as Fargo had done. After a moment he stood and said, "Some of you men get hold of her and carry her up to my office. Moving her isn't going to put her in any more danger, and I can do a better job of cleaning and dressing the wound there."

Several of the bystanders volunteered, and a moment later Roxanne was being carried carefully down the street toward Pierce's office. Fargo and Vance followed behind.

"You're a damned fool," Fargo said under his breath.

To his surprise, Vance didn't argue with him.

"I know," the young man said miserably. "I never should have left the hotel without you, Skye. I just woke up hungry and thought I'd get something to eat. If I hadn't done that, Roxanne wouldn't be hurt."

"I reckon there's a real good chance she'll pull through. But if that bullet had been a few inches to the left . . ."

Fargo shook his head.

After a moment, Vance said, "From now on I'll

do exactly what you say. You have my word on that."

"Good. Right now let's just make sure Roxanne is going to be all right."

They followed the others up the stairs to Dr. Pierce's office. The volunteers gently placed Roxanne on the examining table. Pierce thanked them, then shooed them all out of the room, allowing only Fargo and Vance to remain. He finished cutting Roxanne's shirt away and went to work on the bullet wound.

Half an hour later, the graze had been cleaned out, disinfected with carbolic acid, and bandaged. Roxanne's face was still pale and drawn, but she had regained consciousness. With help from Fargo and Vance, Dr. Pierce shifted her over into bed.

"What happened?" she asked weakly as she looked up at the men.

"I made another error in judgment," Vance said. "I left the hotel, and one of those men who got away yesterday tried to kill me. He missed and hit you instead."

Fargo said, "Actually, he was trying to shoot me when you got hit. But Vance is right about the rest of it."

The doctor regarded them solemnly from the other side of the bed.

"Don't you think it's time you told me what's going on here?" he suggested. "Perhaps I can help."

Fargo nodded toward Roxanne.

"You've already done everything you can, Doc. Well, that's not strictly true. You're going to have to look after Roxanne here after Vance and I have moved on."

"You're going without me?" she said in surprise.

"We don't have much choice," Fargo told her. "You'll need to rest up and let that wound heal for several days at least, before you can travel again. You're sure not up to riding all the way to San Antonio."

Roxanne looked angry and disappointed.

"But if you leave me here, you're taking a chance on somebody else coming after me," she pointed out. "That's why I wanted to go with you two in the first place."

"Nobody's going to bother you here in town," Fargo assured her. He looked at Pierce. "Isn't that right, Doc?"

"Well, I'm still confused, and it appears that no one is going to explain," the doctor said crisply. His expression softened as he looked down at Roxanne. "But your buckskin-clad friend is correct about that, missy. You'll be safe from whatever mysterious forces threaten you as long as you're under my care."

Roxanne looked a little dubious about that, but she didn't argue with Pierce. Instead she turned to Fargo and said, "You're liable to need my help."

"I don't doubt it, but we'll just have to get by without you."

"Well, damn!" she said. "You're gonna be stubborn about this, aren't you?"

Fargo shrugged and grinned.

"I'm afraid so."

"All right," Roxanne said reluctantly. "I don't like it, but I hurt too much to get up and fight about it." She lifted an arm and reached out to catch hold of Fargo's hand. "But you be careful, Skye, you hear me?"

"I will," he promised.

Roxanne glanced at Vance.

"Don't let this young fool get you killed."

Vance flushed and cleared his throat.

"I believe I'm probably older than you, Roxanne," he pointed out.

"Vance, I was *born* older than you."

"Might be right about that," he muttered under his breath.

"Do everything Skye tells you to do. If he says jump, you jump, by God! And if he tells you to stay put, then don't you budge, you understand?"

"I understand," Vance said with a nod.

"Remember that, and you might make it to San Antone alive. Maybe."

Pierce sighed in exasperation. "My God, you people are cryptic." He held up his hands, palms out. "Still, it's none of my business. As long as I get paid for my medical services . . ."

Vance pulled a roll of greenbacks from his pocket and peeled off several of the bills.

"Will this do, Doc?" he asked as he held them out to Pierce.

The doctor's eyebrows rose in surprise. He reached out, took the money, and tucked it into his pocket.

"That'll be sufficient for the young lady's care until such time as she's ready to travel again. Will she be heading to San Antonio as well? There's a stagecoach twice a week."

"Where she goes will be up to her," Fargo said. He gave Roxanne's hand a squeeze and then leaned over to plant a quick kiss on her forehead. "We've got to be riding."

"You haven't had breakfast," she said.

"I'll get some biscuits at the café we can wrap up and take with us."

"Skye . . ." She managed to lift her right arm enough to put her hand behind his neck and pull him down even closer to her. She winced a little at the pain that caused in her left side, but she kissed him anyway, a lingering kiss that made Fargo wish the situation was different . . . a lot different.

"I have a feeling I'll be seeing you again," she whispered when their lips finally parted.

"I have a feeling you're right," Fargo told her.

"What about the other man who got away?" Vance asked. "What happened to him?"

They were riding out of Buchanan a short time later, leading the pack animal and the extra mounts. Fargo took a biscuit from the bag slung over his saddle horn and gnawed off a hunk before he answered his companion's question.

"No telling," he said. "The other man could have died, or the two of them could have just split up. Maybe the other one went to send word to Big Nate while his friend made one last try to kill you."

Vance shook his head worriedly.

"More men are going to come after us, you know."

"I know," Fargo said calmly. "That's why we need to start teaching you how to do a better job of handling that gun."

Vance perked up at that comment.

"Really?"

"Really." Fargo nodded. "We'll ride a while, then find a good place to stop for a spell and get in some practice."

Vance was eager to get started, Fargo could tell. Around midmorning, he angled the Ovaro off the road and led the way across a field.

Fargo stopped, dismounted, and motioned for Vance to do likewise. He pointed toward a tree that stood alone about forty feet away.

"Shoot at that tree."

"Any particular spot?" Vance asked.

"Just see if you can hit the tree," Fargo said patiently.

He held the reins of all the horses while Vance

faced the tree and took a deep breath. Suddenly, Vance grabbed quickly at the butt of his gun and tried to haul it out of the holster.

Instead, the revolver's wooden grips slipped out of his fingers, and the gun thudded to the ground at his feet. He jumped a little, as if afraid that the gun would go off.

"I didn't tell you to make a fast draw," Fargo said, curbing the impatience he felt. "Pick up the gun, put it back in the holster, and try again."

"I just thought I ought to know how to get the gun out in a hurry," Vance explained.

"It won't do you any good on the ground."

Vance nodded and picked up the gun.

"Check the barrel," Fargo added. "Make sure it didn't get any dirt in it."

Vance did so and then holstered the weapon. He faced the tree again, and when he drew this time, he did so more slowly and deliberately. He cocked the gun as he raised it, then drew a bead on the tree and fired.

"What happened?" he asked. "Did I hit it?"

"Nope. You were wide right. You jerked the gun that way when you pulled the trigger."

Vance frowned.

"Are you sure? I would have sworn that I was pointing the gun right at the tree."

"If you were, there'd be a bullet hole in the trunk now. You're welcome to walk over there and have a look for yourself if you want to."

"No, no, I believe you, Skye. Should I try again?"

"Go to it," Fargo said with a nod.

Vance took aim and fired again. For the second time, no bark leaped off the tree trunk to show that he'd hit it. Vance glanced at Fargo, who nodded again. Twice more, Vance fired, and twice more he missed.

"What the hell am I doing wrong?" he exploded angrily.

"For one thing, you're jerking the trigger," Fargo said. "That makes it more likely you'll pull the shot to one side or the other. You need to squeeze the trigger."

"But that's slow."

"Fast doesn't do you a damned bit of good if you can't hit what you're shooting at."

"What else am I doing wrong?"

"Try to think of the gun as part of your hand," Fargo said. "Point the barrel like you're pointing your finger. If you do that, and if you don't jerk the trigger, the bullet ought to go pretty close to what you're pointing at."

"You're sure?"

Fargo smiled. "Nothing's sure in life, Vance. But I'm convinced I'm right about this, anyway."

"All right." Vance reloaded the empty chambers in the gun and took up his stance again. He pointed the Colt at the tree and fired.

This time a chunk of bark leaped from the side of the trunk.

"I hit it!" he exclaimed. Turning excitedly toward Fargo, he went on, "Did you see that, Skye? I hit it!"

"You grazed it," Fargo said with a nod. "Now do it again."

Vance stood a little straighter and seemed more confident as he continued his target practice. Not all of his shots hit the tree, but several did, enough so that he was encouraged.

"I'm getting the hang of it," he said. "I'll be a gunman in no time!"

"Thinking like that will get you killed," Fargo told him. "But if you keep practicing, I reckon sooner or later you'll get to the point where your friends don't have to worry about you shooting them by accident."

Vance practiced for about an hour before Fargo called a halt to it. They had plenty of ammunition, but Fargo didn't figure they should spend any more time than that on each practice session.

Vance was reluctant to quit.

"Next time I'm in a gunfight, it'll be a different story," he vowed as they rode away.

"It'll be different than this, that's for sure," Fargo said. "That tree wasn't shooting back at you."

Vance frowned but said nothing.

Fargo pushed them at a fairly brisk pace the rest of the day. Since they had several extra mounts, they didn't have to stop to rest the horses, only to switch their saddles to fresh animals. The Ovaro, with his boundless strength and stamina, could have carried Fargo all day, of course, but there was no need for that.

They passed through a few small farming villages but didn't stop. Late afternoon found them riding through mostly empty terrain, with only an occasional isolated farmhouse to break the monotony.

Vance looked around nervously.

"Are there any Indians around here?" he asked.

"Might be a Cherokee family or two, but they're not hostile," Fargo replied. "Go west a hundred and fifty or two hundred miles and you'll find plenty of Comanche, and they'd be glad to lift your hair for you. They haven't raided this far east in more than ten years, though. The last big war party to come over this way got shot up pretty bad at the Battle of Plum Creek, a good many miles south of here. Before that, it was different. It would have been worth their lives for a couple of white men to ride through here alone."

"Thank God for civilization," Vance said fervently.

"I reckon."

Vance looked over at Fargo.

"You don't sound convinced, Skye."

"A Comanche will kill you," Fargo said, "but he won't lie to you, at least not very often. Most of the tribes are that way. They mean what they say and say what they mean. That's why it's been so easy for the government to break the treaties with them. The Indians don't understand that a politician's promise isn't worth a hill of beans."

"Surely the Indians aren't blameless in all the conflicts."

"No, they break treaties, too, but it's usually the young warriors who don't go along with what the old chiefs have agreed to. To an Indian, that's not breaking his word."

"Well, I just hope we don't run into any of them."

"I don't expect to," Fargo said.

They made camp for the night in a grove of trees a short distance off the road. Fargo built a small, almost smokeless fire to heat their food while the sun was still up, then extinguished the flames before night fell.

"No point in announcing to the whole world that we're here," he said to Vance. "You'd better get some sleep. I'll take the first watch."

"We're standing guard all night?"

"I think it would be a good idea."

Vance crawled into his bedroll and was soon asleep, snoring softly. Fargo sat on a log with the Henry rifle across his knees. From time to time he got up and walked quietly around the camp. The stars came out, the moon rose, and the hours drifted past peacefully.

When it came time for Vance's turn to stand guard, Fargo touched him lightly on the shoulder. Vance woke up badly, flailing and disoriented. He sat up and opened his mouth to yell something. Fargo's hand clamped on his jaw, silencing him.

"Take it easy," Fargo said sharply. "It's just me."

"Oh." Vance blinked rapidly and shook his head. "Skye. I didn't realize . . . I guess I must have been dreaming . . ."

"Well, it's time to wake up." Fargo put the Henry in Vance's hands. "You're on guard duty now."

"You make it sound like we're in the army." Vance yawned prodigiously.

"There are worse things . . . like being snuck up on by bushwhackers. Are you good and awake?"

Vance nodded.

"I'll be fine. Don't worry."

Fargo wasn't worried much, because the Ovaro was picketed close by and he knew the big stallion was the best natural sentry in the world. If any strangers came around, the black-and-white horse would let him know. Fargo was accustomed to sleeping lightly and trusting to the Ovaro's keen senses.

So it didn't really matter if Vance did his job or not, but Fargo wanted to see how the young man would handle the responsibility. Fargo rolled in his blankets and dozed off quickly.

When he woke up early the next morning, shortly before dawn, he wasn't surprised to see that Vance had fallen asleep sitting up. Vance was leaning against a tree, his eyes closed, his mouth open slightly, dead to the world. Fargo sat up and shook his head.

He got out of his bedroll, pulled on his boots, and put on his hat. He had slept with his gun belt on. After walking silently over to Vance, Fargo abruptly kicked the youngster's foot and reached down to snatch the Henry out of his hands.

Vance came up out of sleep, yelling and cursing. Fargo put a hand on his shoulder and shoved him back down.

"Good thing I wasn't counting on you to keep us alive," Fargo said.

Vance glared at him and then wiped the back of a hand across his mouth.

"I'm not used to living like this," he said in surly tones. "And I'd probably feel better if I had a damned drink!"

"Yeah, a snootful of whiskey would have kept you awake," Fargo said sarcastically. "That's what you need, all right."

"You're a cold-blooded bastard, you know that, Fargo?"

"I never claimed to be anything else. Now get up. We've got places to go and things to do."

Breakfast was a quick affair, bacon and biscuits washed down by black coffee. The sun had been up only a few minutes when the two men broke camp and resumed their journey southward.

Now that Vance had gone more than twenty-four hours without alcohol, he was really starting to feel the effects. He muttered and complained, sweated and rubbed his hands over his face.

"I gotta have a drink," he said.

Fargo shook his head.

"No, you don't. You just think you do."

Vance glared over at him.

"Have you ever had to give up something that was a big part of your life?" he asked peevishly.

Fargo thought back over the losses he had suffered during his life.

"More than you know, Vance," he said quietly. "More than you know."

That quieted the young man's complaints for a while.

Fargo kept them moving at a good pace most of the day. Before it was over, Vance had the shakes and could barely hold the reins.

"I can't go on like this, Skye," he rasped as they approached a larger settlement late that afternoon. "There's bound to be a saloon in that town up yonder. Let me have a beer, anyway. Just a beer, for God's sake!"

"You drink a beer and before you know it you'll have a gutful of whiskey," Fargo told him.

"Come on, Skye," Vance wheedled. "Don't *you* want a drink?"

To tell the truth, Fargo could have used a shot of whiskey to cut the trail dust right about now. But he shook his head and said, "I'm fine. You don't really want that drink as much as it wants you, Vance."

Vance just stared over at him.

"That doesn't make a lick of sense."

"Maybe it will once you've been sobered up for a while."

They rode into the town of Meridian, and since it was as late in the day as it was, Fargo decided they could spend the night at a local inn. He made sure they just got one room, however, so that Vance couldn't sneak out during the night and hunt up a saloon.

Vance didn't sleep well, tossing and turning and muttering, and in the morning he looked like warmed-over death. Felt that way, too, to hear him tell it. Fargo was sympathetic but didn't show it. He kept up the stern, stony façade.

"You'll be all right," he told Vance as they hit the trail again.

"I couldn't even stand to eat this morning," Vance croaked.

"We've got plenty of jerky in our saddlebags for

you to gnaw on if you get hungry before noon," Fargo said.

Vance just groaned.

When they came to a creek later that morning, Fargo paused to let the horses drink. Vance got down from the saddle, went over to kneel beside the stream, and plunged his head under the water. He came up shaking his head and spraying drops of water around him.

Then he started to drink, cupping the cool, clear water in his hands and sucking it down as fast as he could. From time to time he ducked his head under again and then resumed guzzling the water.

Fargo had seen men do that before when they were coming off a long drunk. The whiskey was leaching out of them, and they had to have moisture to replace it.

Vance dried his face on his sleeve, but it was wet with sweat again almost right away. He groaned.

"Fargo, I can't stand this! Damn it, I got to have a drink!"

Fargo stood beside the Ovaro, holding the stallion's reins.

"No, you don't," he told Vance. "You don't know it, but you're already past the worst of it. Just hang on a while longer—"

"I can't hang on, damn you!" Vance roared. He lurched up onto his feet. "Gimme a drink, you bastard!"

And with that he lunged at Fargo, swinging his fists in a desperate attack.

8

The Trailsman stepped aside easily from Vance's rush. Fargo's leg went out, and Vance tripped, landing with a heavy thud and rolling over. When he tried to push himself up, he groaned and collapsed again.

"Better stay put for a minute," Fargo advised. "Your head'll stop spinning if you give it a chance."

Vance cursed him in a low voice, grating out the sulfurous venom.

"I've been cussed out by bullwhackers, Vance, and they're the all-time experts on the subject," Fargo said. "You're just wasting your breath."

Vance finally made it to his knees. He staggered upright, and as he turned toward Fargo, he clawed at the gun on his hip.

That made it serious. Fargo dropped the Ovaro's reins and stepped forward quickly. His left hand shot out to grab the wrist of Vance's gun hand as he started to drag the iron out of leather. A sharp twist made him drop the revolver.

At the same instant, Fargo's right hand moved in a blur, his fist smacking solidly into Vance's jaw. As he stumbled backward, his feet got tangled up with each other, and he went down again, almost falling under the hooves of the horses. The animals shied away.

Fargo bent and picked up Vance's gun from the dust. He checked it and saw that it was clean. Then stood over the groggy young man.

"Most men who try to throw down on me, I just shoot 'em," Fargo said, his voice hard as flint. "I'm working for you, so you get the benefit of the doubt, Vance . . . this time. Don't try it again."

"You . . . you bastard . . ." Vance mumbled.

"And I'm getting a mite tired of being talked to that way, too. Now get up. We've wasted enough time here."

Vance just muttered more curses and stayed where he was, sprawled on the ground next to the creek.

Fargo turned away in disgust, still holding Vance's gun. He stopped short as he looked back along the road and saw dust rising in the distance.

Somebody was coming.

That didn't have to mean anything bad, he reminded himself. He and Vance had seen other travelers during their journey. This was a stagecoach route, too, although it seemed to Fargo that it wasn't time for a stage to be coming along. But he wasn't sure about the stage line's schedule, so he couldn't rule that out.

Nor could he rule out the possibility that more of Big Nate Pryor's hired killers were approaching.

He stuck Vance's gun behind his belt, then bent over and grabbed the young man's shirt with both hands.

"Get up!" Fargo barked as he hauled Vance bodily to his feet. "Somebody's coming, and it might be more of those fellas who want to shoot holes in you."

Vance was unsteady, but he managed to stay upright. He scrubbed his hands over his face, wincing when he touched the spot on his jaw where a bruise was beginning to appear.

"Gimme my gun back," he said.

"Do you plan on trying to shoot me again?"

"No. I'm sorry, Skye. I . . . I just lost my head there for a minute."

Fargo wasn't sure whether to believe the apology was genuine or not, but at least Vance sounded sincere. He handed over the gun. Vance slipped it back in its holster.

"Shouldn't we mount up and get out of here?" he asked.

Fargo shook his head.

"Whoever that is, they're too close to run away from now. Besides, there are enough trees here along this creek to give us some good cover if it comes to a fight."

Vance wiped the back of his hand across his mouth.

"You think it'll come to that?"

"We'll know soon," Fargo said.

Sure enough, it was only a few moments before a buggy and several horsemen came into view, moving down the road at a good clip. The sight of the buggy eased Fargo's worries a little. It seemed unlikely that hired killers would be using such a vehicle.

Fargo and Vance stood by the horses, waiting. As the buggy came closer, Fargo saw to his surprise that the two-horse team was being handled by a woman, and handled skillfully, too.

His surprise grew even greater when Vance exclaimed, "I know that buggy! It belongs to my family. And that's—Oh, my God! That's my sister driving!"

The woman drew the buggy to a halt, and the horsebackers with her reined in their mounts.

Fargo could see now that there was another woman in the buggy. A shock went through him when he recognized Roxanne.

"Skye!" she called happily. "Skye, it's me!"

"I can see that," Fargo said as he walked over to the buggy. Vance came with him.

"Charlotte, what in blazes are you doing here?" the young man demanded of the woman at the reins.

"I'm glad to see you, too, little brother," Charlotte Forrestal said dryly.

She was older than Vance, in her mid-twenties, perhaps, and quite pretty. Dark blond hair was pulled into a bun at the back of her neck, and a blue hat that matched her traveling outfit was perched on her head. She wore black gloves.

Roxanne held out her hands toward Fargo.

"Help me down from here, Skye," she said. "I want to give you a hug."

Fargo didn't grant that request right away. Instead he let his gaze play over the four hard-faced men who accompanied the buggy. Each man wore a holstered Colt and had a rifle in a saddle sheath. Hired guns, he thought, but of a higher quality than those who had come after Vance.

What were they doing traveling with a woman like Charlotte Forrestal?

"Skye," Roxanne prodded.

Fargo stepped over to the buggy and helped her climb down from the seat. She put her arms around his neck and hugged him tightly.

"I know it's only been a couple of days, but I missed you," she said.

Fargo had his left arm around her, but he didn't return the hug for fear of hurting her wounded side. He kept his right hand close to the butt of his gun. Until he knew exactly what was going on here, he would continue to be cautious.

Charlotte answered her brother's question. "I came after you, of course. When Father mentioned that you were on your way to San Antonio to marry that Pryor girl, I couldn't believe you didn't tell the rest of the family."

"Why should I have told any of you?" Vance asked in a surly voice. "None of you cared about me. None of you ever believed in me."

"That's not true!" Charlotte exclaimed. "I always believed in you, Vance. You just wouldn't give me a chance to show you."

Fargo frowned slightly as he listened to the conversation. Vance had claimed that his family had all but disowned him. All Fargo had to go by, though, was Vance's own word for that. Maybe the rest of the Forrestals weren't as bad as he had painted them.

"So you came after me," Vance said to his sister. "Why?"

"To attend your wedding, of course." Charlotte's expression grew more serious. "And to see to it that you got there safely. From the way you talked when you first came back from down there, Sally's father would do anything to stop her from marrying you."

Vance jerked his head toward Fargo.

"That's why I hired Skye here. But I'm sure you've heard all about what happened from Roxanne."

Charlotte looked at Roxanne and said, "Of course."

"Miss Forrestal and her friends came into Buchanan yesterday," Roxanne told Fargo. "They asked the sheriff about you and Vance, and the sheriff came over to Dr. Pierce's to talk to the doctor. That's when I heard what was going on, and I asked the sheriff to introduce me to Miss Forrestal."

Fargo saw the sparkle in Roxanne's eyes. She hadn't liked being left behind, and now she had found a way to remedy that. She was proud of herself.

Fargo wasn't satisfied with all the explanations just yet. He said to Charlotte, "Who are these men, Miss Forrestal?"

"Bodyguards that I hired to come with me," Charlotte said bluntly. "It's a long way from Fort Worth to San Antonio. I certainly wasn't going to make the trip alone. And I thought as well that Vance might need the protection, too, once I caught up to him. From what Roxanne tells me, it was a wise decision, since Pryor's men have already tried to kill my brother several times."

Fargo couldn't argue with that. But he wasn't ready to fully trust these hard-faced gunmen, either.

"So you vouch for them?" he said to Charlotte.

"Of course." She turned her head to look at one of the riders, a tall, weathered man with iron-gray hair under his black hat. "Mr. Trask?"

He dismounted, came over to Fargo and Roxanne, and stuck out a hand.

"I'm Ben Trask, Fargo," he said. "I've heard plenty about you, and I'm glad to meet you."

"Trask," Fargo said as he shook hands. The name was familiar to him for some reason, and after a moment it came back to him. "You're the one who brought that wagon train into Santa Fe after the Pawnees and the Utes went on the warpath. Had to fight almost every mile of the way."

Trask's leathery face creased in a grin.

"That's right. I've guided a few other wagon trains, too, although not as many as you, Fargo." He indicated the men with him. "That's Beaumont, Larribee, and McDade. Good men, all of them."

Fargo relaxed a little. Ben Trask had a good reputation, and if he spoke up for the other three, they were probably all right, too, even though Fargo hadn't heard of them before.

"A job like this seems a mite unusual for you," he commented.

Trask shrugged.

"I was in Fort Worth and at loose ends when Miss Forrestal started looking for men to ride with her to San Antonio. I haven't been down that way in a while, so it seemed like a good idea."

"Mr. Trask was kind enough to find these other gentlemen to come with us," Charlotte put in.

Vance said, "All right, you're here. Now what do we do?"

Roxanne answered before Charlotte had a chance.

"Why, we all travel together, of course. Nobody's going to bother a party this big and well armed."

"That was my thinking exactly," Charlotte said.

What the two women said made sense, Fargo thought. He was still a little uneasy about it, but it was true that any of Pryor's hired killers would think twice about jumping such a large bunch of fighting men.

There were still some concerns, however. He looked at Roxanne.

"Are you sure you're up to that much traveling, even by buggy?"

"Dr. Pierce said I'm healing well and that it ought to be all right as long as the road's not so rough that I get bounced around a lot. The dressing on the wound will need to be changed every day, but I can do that." She smiled. "Or I can get you to help me if I need to, I'll bet."

Fargo didn't comment on that. He looked at Vance instead and asked, "What do you think?"

Vance seemed surprised.

"Me? You're asking me?"

"It's your wedding we're going to," Fargo pointed out.

"Well, yes, that's true." Vance still looked a bit shaky, but his sister's unexpected arrival had distracted him from the miseries he'd been suffering. "I guess . . . I guess it would be all right."

"It's settled, then," Charlotte said briskly. "We'll all go together." She paused. "Vance, you don't look at all well."

"I'm all right," he said. "Just a little under the weather."

"Well, if you say so . . . Ben, are we ready to move on?"

"Soon as we water the horses, Miss Forrestal," Trask replied. He looked at Fargo. "If that's all right with you."

"We're ready when you folks are," Fargo said with a nod.

Ben Trask seemed friendly enough, but Fargo got the feeling that the older man might be just a little resentful of his reputation. Trask had been to see the elephant, too, but Fargo was much better known on the frontier.

Fargo told himself not to borrow trouble. He would keep an eye on Trask and the other three men, and for now that would be enough.

A short time later they were on the move again. Fargo and Vance rode beside the buggy, as did Trask and McDade. Beaumont rode out ahead on point, while Larribee brought up the rear. It was a solid arrangement in case of trouble.

Charlotte's party had a couple of packhorses and plenty of supplies. When the group stopped at midday, they were able to pool their provisions and come up with an excellent meal. This might not be so bad, Fargo thought as he enjoyed a plate of beans, roast beef, and biscuits, washed down by hot coffee and followed by a can of peaches.

Roxanne sat beside him on a log as they ate, her thigh pressed warmly against his. Fargo responded to her nearness, but he knew there wasn't much they could do in the way of romance while that wound in her side was healing.

After the meal, Vance came over to them and said, "We need to get back to my shooting lessons, Skye. I felt too bad yesterday, but I think I could manage again today."

The young man seemed steadier now than he had earlier, Fargo had to admit as he looked up at him.

"I'm not sure I want to teach you any more about gun handling," he said quietly, "considering that you tried to draw on me once today already."

Roxanne's eyebrows arched in surprise at that comment. None of the others heard it.

Vance looked embarrassed.

"I was out of my head then, and you know it," he said. "But you were right. I've turned a corner, Skye. I can feel myself getting stronger now."

Fargo wasn't totally convinced. He knew that Vance could backslide and fall again into his boozing ways very easily. But he also believed in giving people a chance.

"All right," he said. "Hold out your hands."

"Both of 'em?"

"That's right."

Vance extended his hands in front of him. They were fairly steady at first, but then a tremor came into them.

"That's not fair," he said as he lowered them. "Nobody can hold their hands perfectly still."

"That's right," Fargo agreed. "But you're a little shakier than most."

"Damn it, let me try again."

Vance's face screwed up in concentration as he held out his hands a second time.

They were steadier, and each time they started to tremble a little, Vance was able to still the motion. Beads of sweat popped out on his face as he poured a considerable effort into what he was doing. He looked anxiously at Fargo as if waiting for the Trailsman to say that was enough.

Fargo didn't say anything, though, and finally Vance had to drop his hands.

"How long were you going to let me stand there like that?" he demanded.

"As long as you could," Fargo said. "And you did pretty good, too. Let's see how well you can hit a target today."

He stood up and led Vance well away from the buggy. Trask and the others watched curiously. Charlotte called, "What are you doing, Vance?"

"Wait and see," he told her.

About fifty feet away, a rock jutted up out of the ground. It was no more than a foot wide and stood perhaps eighteen inches high.

Fargo pointed at it and said, "Hit that rock."

Vance took his position, shoulders slightly hunched, fingers dangling near the butt of his gun.

"Remember, no fast draws," Fargo warned him. "Just draw and fire, nice and easy."

Vance nodded and took a deep breath. He pulled the Colt from the holster and raised it. His thumb eared back the hammer.

The gun belched flame and smoke as he pulled the trigger.

When he lowered it, the rock was unmarked. He asked, "Did I miss it?"

"Clean miss," Fargo told him. "You shot high."

Instead of cursing, Vance nodded calmly.

"I'll remember that."

He tried again and missed a second time. Fargo waited for the angry, frustrated outburst, but Vance just looked at him and asked, "Was I high again?"

"Just a little," Fargo said.

Larribee sauntered forward. The man had very black hair and a lantern jaw. With a cocky grin on his face, he said, "I'll show you how it's done, kid."

"He's doing fine," Fargo snapped. "He just needs practice."

Something flared in Larribee's dark eyes for a second, but he nodded and backed off readily enough.

"Sure. You go right ahead, kid."

Vance cocked the revolver and took aim again. This time when he squeezed the trigger, the bullet smacked the top of the rock and whined off in a ricochet. He turned and grinned at Fargo.

"You've got it now," the Trailsman told him.

Vance fired the other two rounds in his gun, and both of them were hits. He reloaded, filling all six chambers of the cylinder this time instead of leaving one empty for the hammer to rest on. He emptied the gun fairly quickly, and four of the six bullets struck the rock.

Roxanne applauded and called to him, "That's really good, Vance!"

Fargo glanced at Charlotte Forrestal. She was watching her brother's target practice with great interest, but her lips were slightly pursed with what looked like disapproval. She might not care for the fact that Vance was learning how to handle a six-gun.

For another quarter of an hour, Vance loaded and fired, loaded and fired, and at least seventy-five percent of his shots were hits.

"That's enough," Fargo told him after that. "No need to melt down the barrel."

Vance began to reload again.

"I think I'm doing pretty good," he said.

Before Fargo could agree, Larribee strolled forward again.

"When you get really good, you'll be able to do this," he said.

With that, his hand darted to his gun and drew it, almost too quick for the eye to follow. His left hand swept across and hit the hammer, knocking it back even as the index finger of his right hand squeezed the trigger. The gun roared again and again in a matter of heartbeats as Larribee continued to fan it.

He emptied the Colt, and all five slugs splattered against the rock.

With a glance of triumph at Fargo, as if daring the Trailsman to match that feat, Larribee let the smoke drift from the gun barrel for a moment. Then he began reloading.

"That was good shooting," Fargo said quietly.

"Thanks," Larribee replied with a smug smile. With a little twirl, he slid the reloaded gun into its holster and walked back to join his friends.

"So, Vance, you're practicing to be a gunman?" Charlotte said. Her tone mirrored that disapproval Fargo had seen in her eyes a few minutes earlier.

"No, not really," Vance said. "I just want to be able to protect myself. I've been learning that it's a handy skill to have."

"Of course it is. But you don't really need to go around shooting up the place when you're a businessman, now do you?"

Vance started to look worried.

"You think it's a bad idea, Charlotte?"

"I'm just not sure it's necessary. You have Mr. Fargo and these other gentlemen to look after you."

Fargo was glad to see that Vance's back stiffened a little as he stood up straighter.

"Skye won't always be around, and neither will Mr. Trask and his friends. This is still the frontier, Charlotte, even though civilization is pushing farther west all the time. A man has to protect himself and those who are important to him."

"Can't argue with the boy about that, ma'am," Trask drawled.

"No, I suppose not." Charlotte put a smile on her face, but Fargo wasn't sure how genuine it was. "Just be careful, Vance. You know how you have a tendency to . . . Well, I've said enough, I suppose."

More than enough, Fargo thought. Maybe Vance hadn't been so far wrong about his family after all.

Or maybe Charlotte was just being an overprotective older sister. It was really none of Fargo's business. Getting Vance safely to San Antonio was, and he thought it was about time they started on that chore again.

"Let's mount up and move out," he said.

"Just like bein' back in the army," Beaumont said.

Trask jerked a thumb toward the horses, indicating that they should get moving.

Having the buggy along slowed them down some, but not too much. They would still reach San Antonio in plenty of time for Vance's wedding, Fargo judged. The rest of the afternoon passed peacefully.

They camped near the road that night. Charlotte had brought along a tent, so that she didn't have to sleep out in the open. She insisted that Roxanne share it with her, and although Roxanne cast Fargo a longing look, they both knew that she might as well stay in the tent. They could sneak off for some romping, but it was liable to be too strenuous for that healing wound of hers. The last thing they needed to do was to break it open again.

The next day they stopped at Fort Graham, on a limestone bluff overlooking the stately, slow-moving Brazos River. The Brazos was narrower and faster-flowing farther upriver in the rugged

Palo Pinto country, where Fargo had had a few dustups with Indians and bad men in the past.

Fargo knew the commander at the fort, who assured them that the Comanche had shown no signs of raiding in the area. Patrols rode out from the fort on a regular basis.

The party moved on, the miles and the days rolling behind them. A few days later they stopped at Fort Gates, on the Leon River, and heard the same encouraging message about the lack of Indians from the commanding officer there.

Vance continued to practice his shooting at every opportunity. He had gotten to where he could hit a target nearly every time, and Fargo finally agreed that it would be all right for him to try to increase the speed of his draw.

Vance would never be a truly fast gun—he just didn't have the instincts for it, Fargo knew—but with work he was going to be able to get the weapon out pretty quickly and still hit what he was shooting at.

When they reached the state capital at Austin, on the Colorado River, they stayed in a hotel, much to Charlotte's evident relief. The town, originally a small hamlet called Waterloo, had grown steadily since the capital had been moved there some twenty years earlier from Washington-on-the-Brazos. Texas had been a republic then, a sovereign nation instead of a state.

Fargo had helped Roxanne change the dressing on her wound several times during the trip, and he knew it was healing well. In fact, although still a little tender, it was just about healed by the time they reached Austin. There was no longer any need to keep bandages on it.

Vance was doing a lot better, too. The shakes were gone now, and he was clear-eyed and alert, a far cry from the whiskey-sodden, self-pitying youngster Fargo had first met in Fort Worth.

"Sally is really going to be surprised when she sees me," he said to Fargo as they ate in the hotel dining room that night.

Roxanne reached over and patted Vance's hand.

"She's going to happy to see you, that's what," she said.

Roxanne was wearing one of Charlotte's traveling outfits. No longer a painted-up soiled dove or a pistol-packing frontier gal, she now looked like a respectable, attractive young woman. Fargo found her just as appealing as ever, though.

He wasn't the only one. He had seen the way Larribee and Beaumont looked at her. Trask and McDade were older, and while they might cast an appreciative glance at a pretty girl, they didn't stare at Roxanne with outright lust in their eyes the way the younger men did.

After supper, Fargo got a moment alone with Vance and asked, "Do I need to keep an eye on you tonight, to stop you from sneaking off to a saloon?"

Vance smiled and shook his head.

"I'm going to turn in and get a good night's sleep in a comfortable bed, Skye," he said. "Is my word good enough for you?"

Fargo regarded him intently for a moment and then said, "A week ago it wouldn't have been. Now . . . I think maybe it is."

He put out his hand, and Vance took it, firmly returning the grip.

They all had rooms on the second floor of the hotel. Fargo went to his, uncertain of how he planned to spend the evening. He had been there only a few minutes when a soft knock sounded on the door.

He swung it open and saw Roxanne standing

there, a smile on her face, a bottle of whiskey and two glasses in her hand.

Fargo grinned at her and said, "I was beginning to wonder if you were ever going to get here."

"You think I've recuperated enough for a little exercise?" she asked as she sauntered into the room.

Fargo took her in his arms and used his foot to kick the door closed.

"Let's find out," he said.

9

Once they were both nude, Fargo suggested that Roxanne be on top this time, to protect her injured side, and she agreed. She let out a moan that testified just how agreeable she was as she sank down on his hard shaft, impaling herself on his manhood.

Her beautiful breasts bobbed enticingly as she rode him, hips pumping back and forth eagerly. Fargo reached up and cupped those firm globes of creamy female flesh. His thumbs strummed the pebbled brown nipples. Roxanne gasped in pleasure as Fargo's hips thrust upward, matching her stroke for stroke.

He moved one hand downward, caressing her belly and running his fingers through the dark thicket of hair that covered her femininity. She put her hands on his chest to brace herself and increased the pace, as if riding a horse that was galloping toward the finish line.

That finish would not be long in coming, Fargo knew. There was too much pent-up passion in both of them to tolerate much delay. Later, there would be time for plenty of slow, sensuous lovemaking.

Now he gripped her hips and pounded up into her, feeling his arousal rise higher and higher until his climax burst out of him. Roxanne's culmination gripped her at the same time. Shudders rippled through her. She cried out.

When both of them were drained, Roxanne slumped forward on Fargo's chest. She was out of breath and all her muscles were limp in the aftermath of her climax. Fargo stroked her flanks and buttocks and kissed her neck and shoulder. She slid her arms around his neck and held him tightly.

"You've ruined me, Skye, you know that," she whispered. "I'll never be satisfied with any other man again."

"That's not true," Fargo told her. "When you meet the right fella, it'll all be fine."

"I don't suppose you . . ."

"Once we get to San Antonio and Vance is all squared away, I'll be moving on," he said without hesitation.

She propped herself up on an elbow and looked down at him in the dim light of the lamp they had turned low.

"You're one of those men who never stays very long in one place, aren't you?" she asked. "You always have to be riding on, to see what's over the next hill or in the next valley."

"That's the way I've been living for a lot of years," Fargo said. "It might change someday—I really don't know—but I do know I'm not ready to settle down yet. Any woman who thought I was would be letting herself in for a lot of trouble."

Roxanne laughed softly.

"Don't worry, Skye. I'm not trying to hog-tie you. One thing my life has taught me is to deal with things the way they are, not the way I wish they were."

Fargo brushed his lips across her forehead.

"That's the best way to be."

They lay there like that for a while, content simply to enjoy each other's nearness, and Fargo wasn't particularly surprised when he woke up and realized they had dozed off in each other's arms.

Something had awakened him, though, and after a moment he heard it again: a soft knock on the door of his room.

Roxanne was sleeping soundly, her breathing deep and rhythmic. Fargo didn't want to disturb her. Carefully, he slid out of the bed. Roxanne stirred a little, but then she immediately settled down again.

Fargo pulled on his buckskin trousers, picked up his Colt from the bedside table, and padded barefoot to the door. He didn't figure anybody would be shooting off shotguns in the middle of Austin, so he asked quietly, "Who's there?"

"It's Larribee, Fargo," came the reply. "There's trouble."

Fargo felt a coldness along his spine. Things had been going too well for the past few days, he thought. He had hoped that the rest of the journey would be uneventful, but that was too much to expect.

He eased the door open a few inches and saw Larribee standing tensely in the hall.

"What's wrong?" Fargo asked.

"The kid's gone. His sister says he probably snuck out to go find a saloon and get drunk."

Fargo bit back a curse. He had trusted Vance, and it looked like that had been a mistake. He opened the door farther and stepped out. Vance's room was across the hall. Fargo intended to have a look and see if there was anything there to indicate where Vance might have gone.

It was possible, too, that someone had grabbed him and taken him out of the room by force, although they would have had to be awfully quiet about that not to have caught Fargo's attention, even occupied as he had been with making love to Roxanne.

Larribee stepped back to give Fargo some room. Fargo was moving past the man when a door suddenly opened farther down the hall and a bloody figure lurched out.

"Fargo!" Ben Trask croaked. "Look out!"

Larribee grated a curse and lunged toward Fargo. In the light from a lamp at the end of the hall, Fargo saw a glint of cold steel. He twisted lithely, and metal rang against metal as he used the barrel of the Colt to fend off the knife that Larribee thrust.

Larribee slashed the blade at Fargo's face in a vicious backhand. Fargo ducked underneath. He could have triggered a shot, but he didn't want to kill Larribee. He wanted to take the man alive instead, so that he could find out why a supposed ally had suddenly become an enemy.

He had a hunch the answer had something to do with Big Nate Pryor.

Fargo's foot shot out and swept Larribee's legs out from under him. The gunman fell heavily, and the knife slipped out of his fingers and skittered away on the carpet runner. Fargo took a step back and leveled the Colt at Larribee.

"Hold it right there, you son of a bitch," he grated.

A footstep behind him took him by surprise. He glanced over his shoulder and saw the pale, frightened face of Charlotte Forrestal. He was about to tell her to get back in her room where it was safe when he saw the small fireplace poker clutched tightly in her hands.

She slammed it against the side of his head.

The blow wasn't hard enough to knock Fargo

out, but it sent him staggering against the wall of the corridor as he tried to hang on to consciousness. He lost his balance and went to one knee.

Larribee was on his feet again. He launched a kick that caught Fargo in the belly. Fargo doubled over.

"You bastard!" Larribee said. "I'll kill you!"

"There's no time, and we don't want any shooting!" Charlotte said urgently. "Come on!"

Fargo battled to get up, but his muscles refused to obey his brain's commands. He was stunned, only half-conscious, and only vaguely aware of the sound of hurriedly retreating footsteps.

Then he felt cool hands on his face and heard Roxanne's voice, ragged with strain as she called, "Skye! Skye, are you all right?"

Fargo managed to lift his head. Roxanne knelt beside him. She hadn't bothered to dress but had just wrapped the sheet around herself. Under other circumstances, she would have been mighty pretty like that. As it was, though, Fargo was in no mood to appreciate her beauty.

"Help me up," he rasped.

"Your head's bleeding—"

"Doesn't matter. I've got to get up."

Roxanne got her hands under his right arm, and he braced his left hand against the wall. He lurched to his feet and stood there for a moment, letting his crazily spinning head settle down.

When it had, he looked around. There was no sign of Larribee or of Charlotte Forrestal. Ben Trask sat about twenty feet down the hall, though, his back propped against the wall.

The front of his shirt was soaked with blood.

"Check Vance's room," Fargo told Roxanne. "I'll see about Trask."

"You're all right now?"

Fargo was still a little dizzy, but he nodded.

"Don't worry about me. Just see if Vance is still in his room."

He started down the hall toward Trask, weaving a little at first. His steps were steadier by the time he reached the man's side.

"What happened, Trask?" Fargo asked as he went to a knee.

Trask opened pain-filled eyes and looked up at Fargo, seeming for a moment not to comprehend where he was or what was happening. But then his eyes cleared, and despite the obvious pain he was in, lines of determination appeared on his weathered face.

"Larribee . . . the son of a bitch . . . knifed me . . . didn't see it comin' . . . in time to stop him."

That's what would have happened to him, too, Fargo knew, if Trask hadn't warned him. Larribee would have sunk that knife in his gut, pushed him back in the room, and probably killed Roxanne, too.

Trask was still struggling to speak.

"He thought . . . I was dead . . . didn't know I'm too tough . . . to let a polecat like him kill me."

"That's right," Fargo said. "You hang on, Trask. I'll get help."

Roxanne came up behind them. "Vance is gone, Skye. So are Charlotte, Larribee, Beaumont, and McDade."

Trask's hand fumbled at Fargo's arm for a second, then clutched it with surprising strength.

"They're gonna . . . kill that boy. . . . The gal paid us . . . to do it . . . said he was no-account . . . was gonna ruin her family . . . but after I got to know him . . . and you . . . I couldn't do it . . . Larribee done this . . . to keep me from warnin' Vance."

"Charlotte's the one who paid them to kidnap Vance?"

Trask's head moved up and down in a weak nod.

"Yeah. . . . Reckon she must really hate . . . that brother o' hers. . . . She's been tryin' to kill him . . . all the way from Fort Worth."

Fargo nodded grimly. He wasn't sure of her motive, but it seemed obvious now that Charlotte had been behind the attempt on Vance's life in Fort Worth, as well as Roxanne's kidnapping. After finding out that Vance was still alive, she had recruited more gunmen and set off to see to it personally that her brother wound up dead, biding her time until she was ready to strike.

Those thoughts flashed through Fargo's mind in an instant. He still had unanswered questions, but he knew now who the real enemy had been all along: Charlotte.

"I'll stop her, Trask," he said quietly. "You've got my word on that."

The older man squeezed his arm.

"Much obliged . . . Fargo. Don't waste no time . . . fetchin' a doctor . . . Too late for me . . ."

"Oh, no," Roxanne said.

"I know you'll . . . set things right," Trask whispered.

Then his head leaned back against the wall, and the life went out of his eyes. His hand fell away from Fargo's arm.

Fargo reached up and pressed Trask's eyelids closed. He stood and saw not only Roxanne, but also several other hotel guests standing in the hallway, no doubt drawn by the commotion.

"Somebody go for the law," Fargo said.

"What are you going to do, Skye?" Roxanne asked.

Fargo glanced at Trask's body.

"What a good man asked me to do: I'm going to go after those bastards and stop them from killing Vance."

It took only moments to pull on the rest of his clothes, stomp his feet down in his boots, and strap on his gun belt and the Arkansas Toothpick. He settled his hat on his head as he hurried down the stairs.

As he crossed the lobby, the clerk called out to him, "Mr. Fargo, the sheriff's on the way—"

"The lady can explain everything to him," Fargo snapped. If he waited around for the law, Vance might be dead by the time Fargo caught up to Charlotte and the three gunmen.

Hell, he might be dead already, Fargo thought.

But giving up wasn't in the Trailsman's nature. He stalked out the rear door of the hotel, ignoring the clerk's badgering behind him.

The hotel had a barn and a couple of corrals out back for saddle horses and wagon teams belonging to its guests. Fargo wasn't surprised to see that the buggy belonging to Charlotte Forrestal was gone. So were the horses belonging to Larribee, Beaumont, and McDade.

A sharp call brought the hostler hurrying out of the barn.

"What can I do for you, mister?" the short, wiry, middle-aged man asked.

"A woman and three men just took out that buggy and some horses," Fargo said. He looked over the mounts in the corral as best he could in the darkness and spotted both of the horses that Vance had been riding. "They had a fourth man with them, I figure—"

"Sure, the sick fella," the hostler said without hesitation. "They put him in the buggy and said they were taking him to the doctor. I told the lady there's a sawbones right down the street, but she said they had to take him to a different doctor, one they knew. I helped 'em hitch up the buggy team and saddle the horses, and off they went." The hostler sounded worried as he added, "I didn't do nothin' wrong, did I?"

"Not a thing," Fargo assured him. "Did you see which way they went?"

"Sure. They took off down Congress Avenue toward the river."

That way led south out of Austin. They would probably want to get well away from town before they killed Vance and disposed of his body. That's what Fargo hoped, anyway.

"Thanks. Grab my saddle while I get my horse out of the corral."

"Sure, mister. You goin' after those folks?"

"That's right," Fargo said.

"They weren't takin' that poor young fella to a doctor at all, were they?"

Fargo opened the corral gate and whistled the Ovaro over.

"Just get the saddle," he said.

Minutes later he galloped away from the hotel and headed along Congress Avenue. The land sloped down gradually to the Colorado River. A long wooden bridge crossed the stream, and on the far side of the river, the city street turned into the main road south to San Marcos, New Braunfels, and San Antonio.

There was no guarantee Charlotte and the others would stay on that road, Fargo thought. But they knew that since they had failed to kill him and Roxanne, there would be pursuit following them. Charlotte's plan was ruined. Whatever her goals were, she could no longer accomplish them by killing Vance. The best thing for her to do would be to let him go.

You couldn't expect logic and reason from somebody filled with enough hate to try to have her own brother killed, though. Fargo knew that and knew

Vance was in deadly danger as long as he was in Charlotte's hands.

The Ovaro's steel-shod hooves thundered over the planks of the bridge. Moonlight wavered on the surface of the Colorado River below. Fargo heard flitting and fluttering around him, felt leathery wings brushing against him.

The bats were out tonight, thousands and thousands of them that made their home underneath the bridge and came out every evening to feast on bugs. Fargo gritted his teeth and rode on thankfully leaving the flying varmints behind as the stallion started up the slope on the far side of the river.

Charlotte and her hired gunmen would be moving fast, but their horses weren't fresh and rested. Neither was the Ovaro, of course, but Fargo knew the amazing stamina of the big black-and-white stallion. The Ovaro could bounce back from a day's ride faster than most horses. Fargo urged the horse on, asking for every bit of strength and speed that the stallion possessed.

There were a few houses south of the river, but Fargo soon left them behind. Silvery moonlight washed over the brush-dotted landscape. The road wound between some trees up ahead, and instinct warned Fargo as the Ovaro swept into that stretch of road. He leaned forward suddenly, low over the horse's neck, as Colt flame bloomed in the shadows to the left of the road.

Fargo heard the whine of bullets over his head. He slapped leather and twisted in the saddle to fire his Colt toward the muzzle flashes. A strident yell of pain cut through the night.

Reining in sharply, Fargo whirled the Ovaro to the side of the road. A horseman burst out of the trees on the right and charged toward him. The man had a Henry rifle and fired as fast as he could work the lever.

Fargo went out of the saddle in a rolling dive as slugs sizzled through the space he had occupied a heartbeat earlier. He came up in a crouch and aimed as best he could in the uncertain light. The trees cast shifting shadows across the road.

Everything sprang into sharp relief, though, as Fargo triggered twice and flame belched from the muzzle of his gun. He saw the gunman called Beaumont go flying backward out of the saddle as both of the bullets drilled into his chest. Beaumont hit the road with a thud, bounced once, and then lay still in a shapeless, lifeless heap.

Brush crackled behind Fargo and the Ovaro let out a shrill whinny of rage. Fargo surged up and spun around in time to see the stallion rear up and lash out with his front hooves at the man who had tried to sneak up on his friend and master. The man screamed as the hooves smashed into him and drove him to the ground.

Fargo called off the stallion and raced over. The man still held a pistol, although he was too badly hurt to use it. Fargo's booted foot kicked it out of his hand anyway.

The man's face was covered with blood from a gash in his forehead that one of the Ovaro's hooves had opened up. Fargo recognized him despite the crimson gore and said, "Where did they go, McDade?"

The injured gunman gasped, "G-go to hell, Fargo!"

"You know they murdered Ben Trask, don't you, McDade? Larribee gutted him with a knife. The man you called a friend."

McDade arched his back and clawed at the ground, maybe in pain, maybe in surprise, maybe some of both.

"Ben . . . dead? Larribee said he was just gonna . . . knock him out . . . and tie him up!"

"Larribee didn't want a man like Ben Trask on his trail," Fargo said, his voice flinty. "And don't forget, he and the woman left you and Beaumont behind to deal with anybody who followed them. They left you to die, McDade. Tell me where they were headed, and I'll settle the score for you and Trask."

Fargo spoke quickly, because he knew McDade didn't have much time. He had wounded the gunman, and then the stallion had busted him up good with those flailing hooves. Every time McDade took a breath, Fargo heard a bubbling sound that told him the man was shot through the lungs.

"Hell, I don't . . . know!" McDade gasped. "Headed south . . . is all I know. That gal . . . crazy mad with hate . . . an' Larribee'll do whatever she says . . . long as she promises to let him . . . into her bed . . ."

So it wasn't just money that had led Larribee to betray his friends, Fargo thought. He wasn't particularly surprised.

"Ben's really . . . dead?" McDade said.

"I'm sorry," Fargo told him.

"Well . . . son of a bitch . . . if I'd knowed what Larribee was gonna do, I never would have . . . never would have . . ."

McDade never finished his sentence. The ghastly rattle of his next breath told Fargo he was gone.

Dealing with McDade and Beaumont had slowed him down enough already. Fargo swung up into the saddle and sent the Ovaro galloping down the road again.

Charlotte and Larribee had a lead, but there was no way that buggy could outrun the Ovaro. It might take most of the night, but Fargo would be able to chase them down—unless they turned off the main road onto some side trail. Fargo wished the moon was a little brighter. As it was, all he could do was hope that the fugitives were so desperate to escape that they would stay on the San Antonio road and pour on the speed.

As he swept around a long curve in the trail a few minutes later, he spotted something up ahead, a dark, unfamiliar shape in the road. It took him a moment to recognize it as the buggy, lying on its side. The horses were still hitched to it, but they were frantically trying to pull free.

Fargo didn't see Larribee. In fact, he didn't see anything moving around the buggy except the spooked horses. He reined the stallion back to a walk and drew the Henry from its saddle sheath. He worked the rifle's lever, jacking a round into the chamber.

When he was about twenty yards away, Fargo brought the Ovaro to a halt and stepped down to the road. He walked forward slowly.

"That's far enough!" Charlotte Forrestal's voice suddenly rang out from behind the buggy. "I've got a gun at Vance's head, and I'll kill him if you come any closer, Fargo!"

Fargo stopped where he was. He was accustomed to remaining calm in desperate situations. That ability had helped him stay alive this long. He said coolly, "Take it easy, Miss Forrestal. There's no need for any more killing."

Charlotte gave an ugly laugh.

"The hell there's not! Vance has got to die, or my father will never really see him for what he is— a drunken, no-good bum!"

"I thought your father had pretty much washed his hands of Vance," Fargo said. He wanted to keep Charlotte talking. As long as she was spewing her venom that way, she wouldn't be pulling the trigger.

She laughed again. "My father may say he's through with Vance, but he's not, not really. Be-

cause Vance is his only son. The only one good
enough to take over the business, even though I
know more about running it than he ever will! All
because of that damned thing he's got between his
legs! Hell, Fargo, *I've* got more balls than Vance
ever will!"

Jealousy, Fargo thought. Pure and simple jealousy, that's what was behind this. Charlotte was
older than Vance, but because she was a woman
she thought her father would never trust her
enough to turn over the family business to her.

But he might if Vance was dead.

Fargo shook his head. "You're wrong about
Vance. He's grown up some in the past week or
so. He's not the worthless young drunk he used
to be."

"But don't you see?" Charlotte howled. "That's
even worse! My God, do you think I want him
getting *better*? I just want him dead!"

Fargo changed the subject, hoping to steer Charlotte away from that thought.

"Where's Larribee?"

"That son of a bitch!" she spat. "When the
buggy turned over, he rode off. Said I was on my
own. I paid him, and he abandoned me!" A different tone came into her voice. "I paid him more
than money. Did you know that, Fargo? I wished
it was you I could have gotten to help me, though.
I would have much rather had you than Larribee.
I didn't figure that bitch of a whore would ever let
me near you long enough to convince you, though."

"That would have taken longer than either of us
have left on earth, Charlotte," Fargo said.

"You think so, you bastard? Larribee came
around to my way of thinking quick enough, let me
tell you!"

Fargo took a deep breath.

"Look, Charlotte, it's over. If you kill Vance,

139

you'll go to prison for the rest of your life. You might even hang."

"It doesn't have to be that way," she said. Fargo thought he heard a touch of hysteria edging into her voice.

"Yes, it does," he said firmly. "You haven't killed anybody yourself. Give it up now and you might not even wind up behind bars."

She stepped out from behind the wrecked buggy. Moonlight glinted on the pistol she held in her outstretched hand.

She wasn't pointing the pistol at him, but rather at something, or someone, behind the buggy. It had to be Vance.

"Get on your horse and ride away, Fargo," she said. "I won't kill my brother. He's tied up, and I'll just leave him here. You can come back and turn him loose later, after I'm gone."

Fargo knew she was lying. As soon as he was gone, she would pump that whole cylinder full of bullets into Vance. She was too crazy and filled with hatred to do anything else.

"It won't work, Charlotte," he said quietly. "Put the gun down and walk away from there. Then I'll see to Vance and we'll all go back to Austin."

She shook her head.

"No, I'm not going back. It's too late for that. All your pretty talk doesn't amount to anything. It's just . . . talk."

Fargo had the Henry at his hip. He was pretty sure he could hit her without raising the rifle to his shoulder. But he might not be able to place the shot where he could be sure of not fatally wounding her.

"I don't want to kill you, Charlotte," he said, "and you don't want to die here."

Once more that ugly laugh came from her lips.

"The only one who's going to die is Vance."

"Put the gun down, Charlotte," Fargo warned, sensing that she was gathering her courage.

"Vance . . . and you!" she said, and suddenly she twisted toward Fargo, clearly hoping to take him by surprise.

Fargo couldn't afford to wait any longer. The Henry blasted just a fraction behind the wicked crack of the pistol in Charlotte's hand. Fargo heard the wind-rip of the bullet as it went past his ear.

Charlotte was down, knocked off her feet by the slug as it bored through her body. She had dropped the gun. Fargo ran over to her and went to a knee beside her. She stared up at him, her eyes wide with pain and shock.

"You . . . shot me!"

"You didn't give me any choice," Fargo said. He saw the dark stain spreading rapidly on the midsection of her dress.

"You . . . don't understand . . . I never had any choice . . . either."

With that, her back arched and her lips drew back from her teeth in a grimace. Slowly, she sank back down, relaxing and sighing as death claimed her.

Fargo breathed a curse that sounded much like a prayer. Charlotte Forrestal had brought her own death on herself, just as she had caused the deaths of nearly a dozen men.

But somehow, Fargo still hoped that *El Señor Dios* would show her some of His mercy.

He straightened and stepped over to the wrecked buggy. Vance lay sprawled beside it, his hands tied behind his back, a gag in his mouth. A long coat was draped around him. That was how they had gotten him out of the hotel and pretended he was sick, instead of a prisoner.

He wasn't moving, and for a second Fargo was afraid that the buggy crash might have broken his neck. But a quick check found a strong pulse in the young man's throat. Fargo drew the Arkansas Toothpick and used its keen blade to saw through the thick ropes around Vance's wrists.

Vance came to while Fargo was cutting him loose. He moaned and looked around in confusion, and when his bleary-eyed gaze finally settled on the Trailsman, he said, "F-Fargo? Wh-what . . ."

"Take it easy," Fargo told him. "It's all over."

But as he glanced toward the lifeless shape a few yards away in the road, he wondered if it was really over, or if the pain Charlotte had caused would haunt the Forrestal family for the rest of their lives.

10

"I still can't believe Charlotte was behind all of it," Vance said as he shook his head sadly. "When we were growing up, she . . . she was the one who always took care of me. The big sister who always loved me."

Roxanne reached across the table and took hold of his hand.

"Things change, Vance," she told him. "People change."

"You're living proof of that," Fargo added.

The three of them sat at a table in the hotel dining room, finishing cups of coffee. What remained of their breakfast was on the table in front of them.

It had been a long night. Vance and Fargo had both been checked over by a doctor, who proclaimed them all right except for a few bumps and bruises.

The sheriff of Travis County had gotten into the act, asking questions that had forced Fargo and Vance to go all the way back to the beginning in Fort Worth and explain everything that had happened.

Explaining the what and the how hadn't been that difficult. It was the why that gave them pause, and in the end there was no answer except for the unreasoning jealousy Charlotte Forrestal had felt toward her brother.

The local undertaker had had a busy night gathering up the bodies of Charlotte, Ben Trask, Beaumont, and McDade. There would be an inquest later in the morning, but after hearing the whole story, the sheriff had assured Fargo that it would be just a formality.

Once that was over, Fargo, Vance, and Roxanne could resume their journey to San Antonio.

None of them had gotten much sleep, so they were all tired. Still, Fargo would be glad to put some more miles behind them. He was ready for this trek to be over.

Roxanne said, "So this fella Big Nate Pryor didn't have anything to do with any of the trouble after all?"

"That's right," Vance said. "Charlotte knew he'd get the blame for it, though. That's why she decided to . . . get rid of me when she did. She told me all about it before they knocked me out."

Roxanne shook her head and squeezed Vance's hand.

"I'm sure sorry, Vance. It's a terrible thing."

"Yes," he agreed, "it is."

There didn't seem to be anything left to say. They left the hotel and walked down the street to the courthouse for the inquest.

Just as the sheriff had promised, the proceedings were over quickly, with testimony from Fargo, Vance, and Roxanne establishing what had happened. The coroner's jury returned three verdicts of self-defense and one of murder, that one involving the death of Ben Trask at the hands of the gunman called Larribee. A warrant would be sworn out for Larribee's arrest, but there was no telling where he was by now. He might never be seen in these parts again.

By midday, Fargo and his two young companions were free to go. Fargo, for one, was glad to put Austin behind them.

The line of hills to the west had grown more rugged. It formed the Balcones Escarpment, Fargo knew, called that by early Spanish settlers of Texas because it looked like a long balcony. The escarpment ran all the way to San Antonio, passing a few miles to the northwest of the settlement. The trail would run alongside all the way.

This was pretty country, with numerous fast-flowing creeks and rivers. The three travelers passed San Marcos, with its crystal-clear springs that had provided water for Indians and other pilgrims for longer than anyone could remember. Hundreds of years, at least, Fargo reckoned.

"There are some big caves in those hills," Fargo told Vance and Roxanne as he nodded toward the escarpment. "I've heard stories about them for a long time. Indians lived in them, and owlhoots sometimes used them for hideouts."

Roxanne gave a little shiver.

"I don't see why anybody would want to go underground. Too much like dying, if you ask me."

Fargo just smiled and rode on.

They passed through the town of New Braunfels, founded by German immigrants to Texas. Fargo had been there before and knew where to stop for German beer and sausages and black bread. They spent a pleasant night at an inn there and then moved on.

Two more days of riding would bring them to San Antonio.

Vance was still subdued and upset over Charlotte's betrayal and her subsequent death, but he perked up some as they neared San Antonio, the largest city in Texas and one of the oldest. Along the way he had continued practicing with the six-gun. He didn't have the shakes anymore, and his face had lost its dissipated puffiness and leaned down. He looked like a frontiersman now.

As they rode through the outskirts of town, Vance said, "Thank you, Skye, for everything you've done. I never would have made it this far without you."

Fargo knew Vance wasn't just talking about the trip to San Antonio. He gave the young man a nod and said, "It's been my pleasure."

Their destination was the Menger Hotel, a fancy place built only a year earlier by a local brewery owner. Fargo had been there before; in fact, he'd once had a shoot-out with some hardcases only a block away near the old mission where the rebellious Texicans had forted up to do battle with Santa Anna, back in '36.

The Menger was an impressive two-story edifice of native limestone, its windows and doors decorated with elaborate wrought-iron grillwork. Fargo wasn't surprised that Big Nate Pryor had chosen the hotel for the meeting with Vance. As a man who had come up from hardscrabble circumstances, Pryor now wanted only the best for him and his family.

That didn't include a drunken bum from Fort Worth, no matter how much money the Forrestal family had. No doubt Pryor was going to be very surprised when he met Vance again.

"Doesn't your girl live here in San Antonio?" Roxanne asked as they dismounted in front of the hotel.

"That's right," Vance nodded. "But we agreed to meet here. Neutral ground, so to speak. I'll stay at the hotel until the wedding. You and Skye will, too, of course."

Roxanne blushed prettily.

"Are you sure you want to introduce us to anybody, Vance? I don't know if that would be a good idea."

Vance's answer came without hesitation.

"Of course I'm going to introduce you to Sally. You're my friends, after all. Good friends, both of you."

"We'll try not to embarrass you."

Vance shook his head. "That could never happen."

They went into the hotel, which was every bit as fancy on the inside as it was outside, and registered, with Vance telling the clerk that he was paying for all three rooms. He also paid a porter to take a message to Nathaniel Pryor's house, saying that Vance had arrived at the hotel and asking that Sally and her parents join him for dinner.

"You two are invited as well, of course," he said to Fargo and Roxanne. "And I don't want to hear any arguments about it."

"I'm not arguing," Fargo said with a grin.

"Neither am I," Roxanne said, "although I still think you may be making a mistake, Vance."

"Let me worry about that," Vance said confidently.

He ordered hot water and bathtubs brought up for all three of them. Fargo was grateful for that, as he soaked away a couple of layers of trail dust. He thought about Roxanne, probably soaking likewise, and figured it might have been fun to share one of those tubs with her. Probably not a good idea, though.

They might not have gotten out of there in time for dinner.

As it was, he came down to the Menger's dining room right on time, dressed in clean buckskins. He didn't look that out of place. For all its sophistication, San Antonio was still a frontier town. He wasn't the only man in the dining room wearing buckskins. Nor was he the only one with a gun belt buckled around his waist.

Vance was in a sober black suit, already waiting at a big table in a corner of the room. He stood and shook hands with Fargo, and he was about to say something when he glanced over the Trailsman's shoulder and suddenly seemed dumbfounded.

Fargo turned around to see what Vance was looking at, and he was a mite surprised himself. Roxanne was walking across the dining room, wearing a beautiful cream-colored gown that dipped low off her shoulders. She was as beautiful and elegant as any woman in the room. More so, Fargo decided.

"My goodness," Vance said when Roxanne came up to them. "You look . . . Words can't describe it, Roxanne. You're lovely. Utterly lovely."

"Thank you," she said, blushing again. "You like the dress?"

"It's gorgeous. Where did you get it?"

"I walked around the block to a little shop. I hope it's all right that I had it charged to you, Vance." She added quickly, "I intend to pay you back. Every penny."

Vance shook his head.

"Absolutely not. Your friendship has more than repaid me for anything you might buy, Roxanne." He pulled out one of the chairs and then took her hand. "Here, let me help you."

"Aren't you the gentleman," she said.

Fargo tried not to grin. Vance was seeing Roxanne in a whole new light this evening. But he was only just now noticing what Fargo had seen in her all along. Despite the sordid background she had come from, she was still a lovely, intelligent young woman. She had escaped from that life in time to save herself, and Fargo didn't figure she would ever go back.

A fancy-dressed waiter—what other kind would there be in the Menger Hotel?—brought a bottle of wine to the table. They sipped from the crystal glasses while they waited for the Pryors to arrive.

The wait wasn't a long one. Fargo saw Vance stiffen, and he turned slightly in his seat to watch an older couple and a pretty blonde making their way across the dining room. Nathaniel Pryor was tall and broad shouldered, with a craggy face and thinning gray hair. He looked like he ought to be called Big Nate.

His wife was small, with graying blond hair and a demure manner. Sally Pryor, Vance's fiancée, looked more like her mother than she did her father. Both women were pretty without being beautiful.

Vance and Fargo stood. Vance stepped forward and held out a hand, saying, "Mr. Pryor, it's good to see you again."

For a moment, Pryor regarded him narrowly and didn't make a move to shake his hand. Finally, he gripped Vance's hand and rumbled, "Something different about you, Forrestal."

"Yes, sir." Vance turned to the older woman and said politely, "Mrs. Pryor, it's good to see you again."

She murmured something, and Fargo got the idea that she wasn't the sort of woman who would say much around her husband, preferring to let him do all the talking.

With a big smile on his face, Vance turned then to Sally and reached out to take both of her hands in his.

"Hello, Sally," he said quietly. "I've missed you a great deal." He leaned toward her to kiss her. She turned her head so that his lips brushed her cheek.

That was only appropriate, but Fargo still

thought it was a mite odd. To his way of thinking, a gal who hadn't seen the man she was going to marry for several months would greet him a little more warmly than that.

"Everyone, these are my friends who accompanied me on the trip down here," Vance said, gesturing toward Fargo and Roxanne. "Miss Roxanne Cartwright and Mister Skye Fargo."

Fargo realized he had never heard Roxanne's last name until just now. He was glad Vance had thought to ask her what it was.

"Fargo, eh?" Pryor said as he shook hands. "Seems like I've heard of you. Done some scouting for the army, haven't you?"

"Some," Fargo agreed with a nod of his head.

The women greeted Roxanne much more coolly, especially Sally. Fargo supposed she was a little jealous. Vance hadn't really made it clear just what the relationship was between him and Roxanne.

Everyone sat down, and waiters began to bring over platters of food. An air of awkwardness hung over the table and didn't get any better as the evening progressed. Even though Pryor was somewhat taken aback by the changes in Vance, it was clear that he still didn't like the young man.

Neither, it seemed, did Sally. Vance kept trying to draw her out, but she remained cool and reserved.

Vance and Fargo had discussed it and had agreed not to say anything about Charlotte and the attempts on Vance's life. Vance didn't want to admit to his prospective father-in-law that he had suspected Pryor of trying to have him killed. Now that he had met Pryor, Fargo really wouldn't have put it past him, but in this case, Pryor hadn't had anything to do with what had happened.

When the meal was finished, Vance set his napkin aside. "I suppose now we ought to discuss the details of the wedding—"

"I'm still not sure there's going to *be* a wedding," Pryor cut in. "I've done quite a bit of checking up on you, Forrestal. I'm told that you spend most of your time in saloons, and that your own father doesn't trust you."

"Not anymore," Vance said, adding quickly, "I mean, I don't spend my time in saloons anymore. As for my father trusting me . . . Well, perhaps he doesn't know me quite as well as he thinks he does."

"What does that mean?" Pryor asked with a scowl.

"It means that I've changed in recent weeks," Vance said. "I'm not a drunk, and I intend to work hard and do right by your daughter, sir."

Pryor snorted in contempt and shook his head.

"Once a drunk, always a drunk," he said. "The first thing that goes wrong, you'll crawl right back into a whiskey bottle."

Vance flushed angrily and started to say something, but before he could, Fargo spoke up.

"Pardon me for butting into something that's not really any of my business, Mr. Pryor," he said, "but you've got Vance all wrong. He's straightened up, and he'll do to ride the river with."

Vance turned to look at him.

"You mean that, Skye?"

"I sure do," Fargo said with a nod.

"Normally I'd place quite a bit of weight in anything you had to say, Mr. Fargo," Pryor said. "But I think I know this young wastrel better than you do, and I say he's no good." He pushed back his chair and started to stand up. "Martha, Sally, come on. We're leaving. It's settled. There won't be any wedding."

Vance shot to his feet.

"Hold on just a damned minute! You can't just come in here and tell me that I'm not marrying

151

your daughter, when she's already accepted my proposal."

"That's exactly what I'm telling you."

Vance looked at Sally.

"Sally, say something! Tell your father he can't do this."

She looked uncomfortable, but she didn't say anything.

Frustrated, Vance turned back to Pryor.

"What can I do to convince you you're wrong about me?"

"Not a blasted thing." Pryor turned away and motioned for his wife and daughter to come with him.

Vance reached out and grabbed his arm, jerking him around.

"You can't—"

"Get your hands off me, you little bastard!" Pryor roared. His big, knobby right fist looped up suddenly and smashed into Vance's jaw, throwing him back against the wall.

Fargo wasn't a bit surprised by Pryor's reaction. Fancy clothes and a lot of money didn't always change the man inside. Big Nate had just shown his true colors.

"Skye!" Roxanne exclaimed. "Aren't you going to do something?"

Fargo reached for the wine bottle and poured a little more in his glass. He smiled.

"No need," he said.

Vance leaned against the wall for a moment, lifted a hand to his jaw and worked it back and forth. The dining room had fallen silent, and every eye in the place was on him.

With a roar of his own, he came away from the wall and lunged at Pryor. A hard right and a left jerked the older man's head back and forth and staggered him. While Pryor was off balance, Vance tackled him, driving him backward. Both men fell onto a neighboring table, shattering the legs and sending it to the floor with a tremendous crash.

People yelled and scrambled to get out of the way.

Pryor threw Vance off and went after him, swinging roundhouse punches. Vance fended them off and slugged back. They went down again, rolled and wrestled on the floor in the wreckage of somebody's meal, and came up toe to toe, whaling away at each other.

Martha and Sally Pryor stood by watching in horror, their hands pressed to their mouths.

At the table, Roxanne held out her glass to Fargo for more wine.

"Now I understand," she said. "And I ain't a bit . . . I mean, I'm not a bit surprised. Vance is a whole different fella from the one who left Fort Worth."

"That he is," Fargo said with a nod.

The savage brawl went on for several minutes and probably seemed to last longer than it really did. Both men were tired, but Vance was younger and fresher. He saw an opening and reacted quickly, shooting out a punch that landed squarely on Pryor's jaw and sent the older man flying backward. Pryor crashed to the floor again, and this time he didn't get up for a long moment.

When he did, he held out a hand toward Vance and shook his head.

"That's enough," he said. "I reckon you've proved yourself, young fella."

"Proved what?" Vance snapped. "That I'm good enough to marry your daughter."

"That's right." Pryor's bloody, puffy lips curved in a grin. "That's exactly what I mean."

Realization dawned on Vance's own bruised, bloody face, and he turned expectantly toward Sally . . .

"No!" she cried. "Dear God, no! I'd never marry you!"

Vance stared at her, obviously unable to comprehend what he was hearing. Fargo wasn't all that surprised, though, having seen the way Sally had treated Vance all evening. She didn't like the new Vance Forrestal. Maybe, Fargo thought, because she realized that she wouldn't be able to keep him firmly under her thumb.

"Sally, I . . . I can't believe this," Vance said. "After all we've meant to each other, all the promises we made . . ."

"You're not the man I fell in love with," Sally sniffed. "You've turned into some sort of *ruffian.*"

Roxanne shot to her feet, eluding Fargo's half-hearted attempt to catch hold of her dress and restrain her.

"How dare you talk to him like that?" she demanded as she glared murderously at Sally. "Sure, he wasn't really worth much when he left Fort Worth, but he's changed. He's a good man now, as good as you'll find. Too good for the likes of you, you prissy little . . . little . . ." Roxanne couldn't find the words, so she settled for saying, "You talk bad about him and I'll scratch your eyes out!"

Fargo couldn't help but grin. Things were going very well. He couldn't have planned it any better . . .

That was when he glanced across the dining room and saw a couple of familiar faces at the entrance. Somebody let out a startled yell, and light from the fancy chandeliers suddenly glinted on gun barrels.

"Down!" Fargo shouted as he came up out of his chair, his right hand streaking to the Colt on his hip. His left shot out, clamped on Roxanne's shoulder, and shoved her to the floor, out of the line of fire.

Larribee and another man opened fire from across the room, heedless of any innocent bystanders who might be in the way of their lead. Fargo had to hold off, waiting for a clear shot, as Nate Pryor grabbed his wife and daughter and dragged them to the floor, too. Bullets whipped past Fargo's head and thudded into the wall behind him.

From the corner of his eye, Fargo saw Vance's hand dart under his coat and come out holding a revolver.

"Take the one on the left!" Fargo said.

Vance nodded, and as the last of the diners hit the floor, he and Fargo fired at almost the same instant, the sounds of their shots blending into one.

Vance's man was thrown backward, blood spurting from his throat as the bullet tore through it. Fargo had aimed at Larribee, and the gunman staggered under the impact of the Trailsman's slug. Larribee stayed on his feet, though, and yelled, "Damn you, Fargo! You ruined everything!" as he tried to bring his gun to bear for another shot.

Fargo's Colt bucked in his hand as he fired again. This time the bullet struck Larribee in the forehead, just above his right eye. He went down hard, dead before he hit the floor.

Side by side, Fargo and Vance strode across the room toward the men they had just shot. Smoke curled from the barrels of their guns.

Both of the attackers were dead. Fargo recognized the second man as the last member of the gang that had kidnapped Roxanne, the one whose shoulder he had broken with a shot from the Henry rifle while the man was holding the horses. He had been firing left-handed, since his right was still in a sling and useless.

Somehow, he had joined forces with Larribee, and they had decided to seek revenge on Fargo.

That plan hadn't worked out too well for them.

Fargo holstered his Colt and looked around the dining room.

"Anybody hurt?"

There didn't seem to be, other than the two dead men. Pryor helped his wife and daughter up. Both of them were crying hysterically.

Roxanne came over to Fargo and Vance. She went to Vance first and asked, "Are you all right?"

He nodded as he put the gun back in the cross-draw rig on his left hip, under his coat.

"I'm fine," he said. He put a hand on her arm. "What about you?"

"Not a scratch," she told him. Almost as an afterthought, she turned to look at Fargo. "Skye? . . ."

Fargo nodded.

"Don't worry about me," he said, and meant it. The way things had worked out, he was just fine.

He left a note for each of them, saying good-bye. They had already worked it out the night before, in the Menger's barroom after the brawl and the shooting, that Roxanne would go back to Fort Worth with Vance on the stagecoach. If folks wanted to think she was somebody he had met in San Antonio, that was all right. If anybody remembered her from her days at the Top Notch Saloon and wanted to make something out of it, that was just too damned bad. Vance would put a stop to it in a hurry. Further than that, though, they hadn't made any plans.

But Fargo had a pretty strong hunch about how it would all work out, and early the next morning, riding the Ovaro and leading a packhorse, he rode out of San Antonio, heading west into the hill country.

It was a beautiful day, and he was ready to see what was on the other side of the next rise.

LOOKING FORWARD!

**The following is the opening
section of the next novel in the exciting
Trailsman series from Signet:**

THE TRAILSMAN #287

CALIFORNIA CAMEL CORPS

*Fort Defiance, Arizona, 1857—Skye Fargo
has been hired to help lead a camel
caravan to California for the U.S. Army.
The camels are bad enough. The Navajo
and the killers are much worse.*

Skye Fargo watched as the four horses ran full-out
toward the distant finish line.

One of the Indian ponies had fallen back, but
the other, a pinto ridden by Short Knife, was moving up. It was about to pass the little roan ridden by
a trooper named Logan, and when it did, it would

certainly overtake the leader, a bay with Corporal Slater in the stripped-down saddle.

Fargo took in the scene, the flying hooves of the straining horses kicking up clods of dirt, distorted a little in his view by the heat waves rising from the ground; the riders leaning forward, low over the necks of their mounts almost as if whispering some secret instructions in their ears; the crowd of men waving their arms, yelling, and jumping around to urge their favorite on.

It was a scene that had been repeated for many years. Before the Americans had come into this part of the country and founded Fort Defiance, the Indians and Spanish had met at a spot that was surprisingly green thanks to its flowing springs. There they traded horses, raced them, and gambled on the outcome. After the arrival of the Americans, the tradition had continued, though somewhat uneasily, as the Navajo trusted the Americans even less than they trusted the Spanish.

And Fargo thought that they might have had good reason. His lake-blue eyes narrowed as he saw that Logan had edged his horse dangerously close to the pinto.

Short Knife's attention was concentrated only on the horse in front of him. He had no idea that Logan was so close, and getting even closer.

Fargo wasn't the only one who saw what was happening, however. The cheering that had been coming from the Navajos changed abruptly into shouts of warning, and the yells of the soldiers dropped in volume as they craned their necks to see if the apparent collision would actually occur.

It did. The roan bumped the pinto, but instead of merely nudging the pony off stride, the roan somehow managed to trip it, causing its legs to tangle. The pinto went down in a dust cloud, throwing Short Knife forward.

The Navajo somersaulted once, then rolled and lay still as the roan thundered past, its hooves barely missing his head.

While nearly everyone else ran to see if Short Knife was dead and if the pinto had broken a leg in its fall, Fargo remained where he was, watching the end of the race.

Not that there was any doubt who would win, not now. Slater's horse increased its lead over the other two, and in fact Logan seemed to have no interest in winning. Fargo wondered if he had bet on Slater.

"He can always claim it was an accident," said a gravelly voice behind Fargo.

Fargo turned around to see who'd spoken. It was Carter, a career sergeant who looked as if he'd been in the desert far too long. His face was burned dark brown where it wasn't covered by a bristly gray beard, and his skin was crosshatched with wrinkles. He had developed a permanent squint that made him look as if he was always peering off into the distance. He was a head shorter than Fargo, and skinny as a rake.

"Might get away with callin' it an accident, too," Carter said. "Be hard for anybody to prove any different."

"But you don't believe it was an accident," Fargo said.

"Hell, no. Not any more than you do." Carter pointed a skinny finger. "See there? Slater's crossed over the line. There'll be some boys won money or silver on his ride, and they'll side with Logan, no matter what he says."

"What about the Indians?"

"Hell, what can they do? They ain't about to start anything here. They're outnumbered and out-gunned. Kin' hozhoni, now, he might be a different story."

Kin' hozhoni was better known as Manuelito, one of the Navajo chiefs, a man who'd given the army a certain amount of trouble in the past and figured to continue to do so.

"Manuelito's not here, though," Fargo pointed out.

"No," Carter said. "He's not." The sergeant spit into the dirt at his feet and wiped his mouth with the back of his hand. "But it just so happens that Short Knife's his cousin. What do you think about that?"

"I think we'd better go see if Short Knife's all right," Fargo said, and the two of them started in the direction of the fallen man.

By the time they got to him, the other Navajo men had surrounded Short Knife. They were muttering words that Fargo couldn't quite make out, but he knew they weren't friendly expressions of peace and brotherhood. Fargo and Carter wouldn't have been able to break into their circle even if they'd wanted to, which they didn't.

"They're tryin' to calm him down," Carter said. "Even if he's hurt, he'll be mighty mad about what happened. But, like I said, they don't want a fight."

"Do you?" Fargo asked.

"You must be jokin', Fargo."

They walked past the ring of men over to where Logan stood beside his winded horse. Several other troopers stood nearby, but most of them had gone farther on down to the finish line where they were congratulating Slater on his victory.

"Did you see what that son of a bitch did?" Logan said to anyone who would listen. "Tried to bump me out of the race. Serves him right that his horse stumbled and fell."

Fargo looked at Carter, who shrugged. "I told you he might could get away with callin' it an accident, but I never thought he had the brass to blame it on the Indian."

"You think anybody believes him?"

"Hell, no. But ain't nobody gonna call him on it." Carter cut his eyes at Fargo. " 'Less you do."

Fargo didn't want to get involved in an argument that wasn't really any of his business. He was at Fort Defiance as a civilian employee, and he wasn't there to settle disputes between the fort and the Indians. He'd been hired to do the kind of job he did best, which was to lead a party from here to there through the toughest terrain and help everyone arrive safely at the end of the trail. Because of his ability in that kind of job, he'd earned the nickname of the Trailsman, and his work had led him to Fort Defiance to help lead an expedition. But he had to admit that it was the strangest job he'd ever taken on.

"We oughta check out the Indian's horse," Carter said.

Fargo walked over to where the animal stood. It hobbled away at his approach, but he could tell that it wasn't seriously hurt. The Navajos had probably already decided that. They weren't likely to neglect a good horse, even when a man was injured.

"The horse will be all right," Fargo said.

Carter looked the animal over and nodded. "I believe you're right." Then he glanced up and said, "Well, there comes Slater. He looks plumb satisfied with the whole thing, just like he didn't know what happened behind him."

It was possible that Slater really didn't know what had happened, Fargo thought. He'd been in front of the other two horses, and he couldn't have seen what was going on. On the other hand, it was also possible that Slater and Logan had worked something out between them before the race.

Even if they had, Fargo told himself, it was still none of his business. He heard shouting behind him and turned to see what was happening.

Short Knife had broken through the ring of men who surrounded him and was running toward Logan. He was holding a knife, and his face was twisted with hate.

"Goddamn it," Carter said.

"I thought you said the Indians didn't want a fight."

"*They* don't, but it sure as to God looks like Short Knife does. We gotta stop him."

Fargo thought that *we* was the wrong word, and he wasn't even sure who Carter intended to stop, since Logan seemed well aware of what Short Knife was up to. He even seemed to welcome it, having broken into a big grin when he saw the Indian charging in his direction. Fargo's first instinct was to stay out of it, but when Carter broke into a short-legged trot, Fargo followed him. And then overtook him. Fargo's legs were a lot longer than Carter's, and the Trailsman was more accustomed to exercise that didn't involve riding a horse.

Fargo hadn't gotten far when he realized why Logan was grinning. He hadn't been carrying a weapon when he'd ridden in the race, of course, but at some time since he'd dismounted, someone had given him a pistol. He was holding it casually now, but Fargo could tell he was just waiting for Short Knife to get a little closer.

Short Knife either didn't see the pistol or didn't care. His friends were running after him in an attempt to head him off, but Fargo could see that they weren't going to be able to get to him in time.

So Fargo figured it was up to him.

He was closer to Logan than anyone, and he approached him from the right side. When he was about ten yards away, he called out, "Logan!"

The trooper, surprised, turned to see who was yelling. Fargo's long strides had propelled the Trailsman across the ground between them by that time. He grabbed Logan's wrist with both hands, twisted hard, and pulled down. The pistol fell to the ground.

Logan was infuriated. He hit Fargo in the side of the head with his left fist. Fargo was stunned, but he hadn't let go of his wrist. He shook his head to clear it, then whirled around, swinging Logan like a bag of meal before letting him go.

Logan tried to keep his feet, but he couldn't quite manage it. He danced across the ground for a few yards and fell on his stomach before skidding to a stop. He pushed himself up and started to jump to his feet, but Carter said, "Stay right there, Trooper."

Logan looked around to see who'd called out, and when he saw Carter, his face reddened. But he stayed where he was.

Short Knife had reached Fargo by that time. "You should not have done that."

"He was going to shoot you," Fargo said. "I didn't think that was a good idea."

"He cheated me. He caused my horse to fall. He could have killed me. And the horse. It is a matter of honor that we should fight."

"I'm sorry I got in the way," Fargo said. "But he had a pistol, and you didn't. I don't like the idea of people getting killed, even when it's a matter of honor."

Short Knife was tall, with shoulders almost as broad as Fargo's own. He had dark, angry eyes under heavy, ridged brows, and his black hair was held in place by a braided leather band that went around his head. He shoved his knife back into its leather scabbard and said, "Then you do not understand honor."

"Maybe not," Fargo agreed. "But I understand killing, and I don't like it. It usually just brings more trouble and killing along with it. You don't seem to be hurt too bad, and your horse is going to be fine. Why don't you forget this ever happened and go on home."

Short Knife looked at him with contempt. "I will never forget. I have been cheated." He looked around at the other Navajos who had now joined him. "My friends have been cheated."

"Nobody's been cheated," Carter said. "There won't be any payoff on the race. I'm disqualifyin' everybody."

"You can't do that!"

Slater had reached the group by that time. He was a small man, not much bigger than Carter, just the right size to be riding in a horse race where a couple of pounds in a man's weight made a big difference. He didn't like the idea of disqualification at all.

"I won the race fair and square," he said. "You can ask anybody."

He didn't mean that, Fargo knew. He meant, "You can ask any of my friends."

"I don't see what the problem is," Slater continued. "I crossed the line first. That's all that matters."

Carter turned to look at him. "Maybe that's because you didn't see what happened."

"No," Slater said. "I didn't, but it doesn't matter.

Like I said, I crossed the finish line before anybody else. That makes me the winner."

"No, it just makes you the one who crossed the line. There was an accident, and Short Knife's pony fell."

"It wasn't an accident," Logan said. "He tried to bump my horse, and his own mount wound up falling. It was his own fault that he lost. You can't blame Slater for it."

If two of Short Knife's friends hadn't reached out and taken hold of his arms, he would have jumped on Logan then. As it was, he strained against the hands that held him. The cords in his neck stood out, and a vein throbbed in his forehead.

"Nobody's at fault," Carter said, not looking at Fargo. "We're just gonna call this whole thing off and forget about it. Short Knife's gonna go home, and in a few weeks we'll have another race. And nobody's horse better fall down."

"I won't be here in a few weeks," Slater said. "I'll be headed to California."

"So will I," Logan said.

"Yeah," Carter said. "I know. That's just too damn bad, ain't it. Now break this up and let's forget about it."

One look at Short Knife's face was all Fargo needed to know that the Indian wasn't going to forget anything. And the Trailsman didn't think Logan or Slater would, either.

"It's a long way to California," he said to Carter a few minutes later, after the soldiers and Indians had finally gone their separate ways. "I wish Logan and Slater were staying here."

"I think it's better that they're goin'. That way we won't be riskin' another Indian war every time there's a horse race."

"I don't think there'll be any more races for a while, not the way Short Knife's feeling. They won't be coming back here."

"I can't help that, and maybe it's a good thing, anyway. You and I won't be around to worry about it. We'll be heading off to California. With those damn camels."

Fargo had tried not to think of the camels. He was regretting that he'd taken the job of leading the expedition to California.

"I wonder how a camel would do in a race with a horse," he said. "You ever ride one?"

"Hell, no," Carter said. "I hate those sons of bitches."

No other series has this much historical action!

THE TRAILSMAN

Available wherever books are sold or at
penguin.com